DEVIL MAY CARE

DANGEROUS LIAISONS   BOOK 3

BESTSELLING AUTHOR
ANDREA PICKENS

CHAPTER 1

"Well, well." One of the gentlemen seated at the gaming table glanced up from his cards as a tall, black-clad figure sauntered out of the shadows. "Look what got spit back from the darkest depths of smoke and brimstone."

Chortles from the other players greeted the quip.

"I heard you were dead," continued Lord Osborne. "Or did Satan tire of your caustic humor and decide to return you to the land of the living to plague the likes of us for a few more years?"

Jack Greeley, Viscount Leete and heir to the Hendrie earldom, inclined an ironic bow. "So it would seem." The flickering wall sconces of the gambling den, their oily light muted by the haze of cigars and brandy fumes, caught the amused arch of his dark brows. "You call this the land of the living, Jamie? To me, it appears I have merely exchanged one Hell for another."

"Ha, ha, ha, Jack. You always did have a clever tongue." One of James, Lord Osborne's companions waggled a half-empty bottle and motioned for him to take a seat. "Care to join us in a round of devilry?"

"Perhaps later," replied Jack, "For now, I think that I will simply continue strolling around with my own demons." He held out his empty glass to be refilled. "I shall try to keep them on a leash."

As the laughter died away, he moved on, slowly circling back to the dimly lit salon where games of dice were played. The sharp rattle of the bones punctuated the low groans and louder exultations rumbling through the air. The room hung heavy with a fugue of sweat and desperation.

Slouching a shoulder to the sooty wall, Jack stood for some minutes watching the flashes of ivory tumble across the green baize.

Back from the dead. Yes, by all rights he should have shuffled off his mortal coil. A grievous saber wound suffered on the battlefield in Spain eight months ago would have sent him to his Maker, but a French burial party had spotted a faint sign of life and carried him back to their camp along with their own wounded officers. For weeks, he had felt no will to live, wracked with guilt for failing to reach his cousin in time to save him from an enemy saber. But the lovely Camille, wife of the regiment's commanding officer, had coaxed him—nay, cajoled, bullied, tormented him!—into embracing light over dark.

Lifting the glass to his lips, Jack took a long swallow and let the brandy burn a trail down his throat.

However, in a serendipitous twist of Fate, it turned out that his cousin had also survived. A wry smile tugged at his mouth. Lud, what a reunion *that* had been! The letter explaining his stroke of luck and his imminent arrival home had not reached England, and when he had walked through the door of his father's estate, he had nearly shocked his family and all the household servants into their graves.

The happy occasion had been followed by an even happier event—his cousin Rafael had kindled a romance with Jack's childhood friend, the spirited daughter of a duke who was nursing some painful wounds of her own. The courtship hadn't been easy, but Love—and the sinfully seductive chocolate confections that Rafael created in Hendrie Hall's kitchen—had triumphed over adversity and the scheming of a smarmy fortune-hunter. To everyone's delight, the couple had recently been married.

Love. Jack drained the rest of his drink in one gulp. "Thank God," he muttered through clenched teeth, "that my hide is far too thick for Cupid's flimsy arrow to pierce."

As if to make a mockery of such hubris, the gaming noises stilled for a moment, allowing a snatch of French conversation to drift out from one of the side alcoves at the far end of the room.

Jack pricked up his ears. Had he heard right or was it merely a figment of his own tangled desires?

Camille was wed to another, he reminded himself. *And she was, by virtue of her birth, his country's sworn enemy.*

"Time to move on," he growled under his breath. But his boots seemed nailed to the rough-planked floor.

The voices sounded again, unmistakably Parisian in accent.

Damn. Damn. Damn.

As James made to pass by him on the way to the privy, Jack shifted his stance and gave a casual nod at the alcove. "Who are the Frogs, Jamie?"

"Comte Amirault and his coterie," answered his friend. "The latest faction to gain leadership over the émigré community here in Town." James made a face. "Why our government thinks the Royalists are any use in the war effort is beyond me. It seems they do naught but squabble among themselves and squander their funds on drink and debaucheries."

"That," murmured Jack, "is rather like the pot calling the kettle black."

"True," agreed his friend with a faint grin. "But at least the money I fritter away is my own. I'm not a leech on our government's finances, nor do I make any pretenses of being qualified to participate in international politics."

"Napoleon's days seem numbered. The monarchy will likely be restored in France, so the Royalists may be more important than you think."

James uttered a rude rejoinder, and continued on his way, leaving Jack to stare pensively at the shadowed corner. But as several new players joined the play at the dice table, the noise grew more raucous, making it impossible to hear anything more from the alcove.

Abandoning his vantage point, Jack went off to fetch another drink, which he quaffed even more quickly than the last one. The brandy brought only a headache, rather than the hoped-for oblivion. Suddenly tired of the slurred shouts and flushed faces all around him, he shouldered his way to the side door and let himself out into a narrow alleyway.

A mist was swirling and the stench of decay from the surrounding rookeries pervaded the damp air. Jack turned up the collar of his coat and was just starting to make his way through a passageway at the rear of the building and out to one of the criss-crossing streets when a flutter of movement near one of the iron-banded back doors caught his eye.

A lone person, moving furtively along the wall.

The middle door opened a crack, and a hurried exchange of words, too low to make out, tumbled into the gusting breeze. *A quarrel or a deal gone bad?* By the look of the gestures, the cloaked creeper was angry.

It was no concern of his, and yet he slid into a shallow recess set into the bricks and went very still, all senses on full alert. Something seemed off about the encounter—he couldn't quite put a finger on what it was, but war had taught him to trust his instincts.

Shoulders hunched low, the person turned abruptly as the door drew closed and flitted closer, stepping quickly yet gracefully through the muck. A glance right and then left, then a tug as the voluminous cloak's hood slipped slightly.

Jack felt as if a sudden punch had knocked the wind from his lungs.

"*Sacre Coeur.*" The person was now close enough for the whispered oath to caress his ears.

He shot out a hand, catching hold of the cloak, then quickly muffled the cry about to burst forth from the lady's throat.

Oh, yes. It was *a lady.*

"Stop struggling, Camille," he growled. "It's only me."

"Jack!" She pronounced it "Jacques," drawing out the sound like melted toffee. Her voice—a low siren's lilt that tickled over his skin like a swirl of smoke—made it sound ever so much more exotic than the stolid English syllable.

"*Mon Dieu*, I never expected to encounter *you* here in London."

"Be damned glad you did, rather than one of the murderous cutpurses who lurk in this area," he growled. "Bloody Hell, what are you doing skulking around Lucifer's Lair? These stews are dangerous."

"I—"

Jack cut her off. Now that he had recovered from his initial shock, a myriad of other questions were whirling in his head. "And what the devil are you doing in England? I cannot fathom—"

"Shhh." Her fingers touched his lips. "Please, we cannot talk here. I must be gone."

Though she tried to shake off his grip, he held firm. "I'll escort you to wherever you are going."

"No! I—I can't explain now, but you can't. It would be too risky."

"Pierre—" he began.

"It's on account of Pierre that I am here," countered Camille. "And every moment I linger here puts him in further danger."

He hesitated, torn between duty and the note of desperation in her tone.

"I will be fine, Jack—I beg of you to trust me on this."

"Very well. But only if you promise to meet me somewhere on the morrow to explain."

"There is a coffee house on the west side of Red Lion Square. Be there at noon." With that, she twisted free and like an underworld wraith darted off to become one with the shadows.

Drawing a ragged lungful of the foul air, Jack realized his heart was hammering hard enough to crack a rib. He leaned back against the wall, and slowly reasserted control over himself.

Turn and run—dismiss the chance encounter as a figment of my overwrought imagination.

Reason warned that whatever mystery was afoot, he would be treading on dangerous ground to pursue it.

Jack looked up at the hide-and-seek stars winking through the scudding clouds and uttered a low oath. In French.

Ah, but when have I ever listened to reason.

Miss Harriet Farnum peered out the carriage window as the wheels rolled to a halt. "It's the usual schedule for this week's meeting, Ellie. Meet me back here in two hours."

Her maid nodded, though a shadow of unease flitted over her face. "Your father would have my guts for garters if he knew I let you hare off in this part of Town by yourself."

"No he wouldn't," she assured, stretching the truth just a tad. "He knows that I'm capable of looking out for myself." A diplomat's daughter who had experienced a number of exceedingly rough-and-tumble places during her foreign travels, Harriet had little patience with the rules of Polite Society. Unlike most well-bred ladies, she chafed at the restrictions requiring her to live within a gilded cage. "And besides, he accepts that I have a mind of my own and there's little point in trying to stop me from doing something which I am determined to do."

Ellie repressed a snort. "Aye, I'm well aware of that. But he expects me to exercise some degree of restraint."

"No, he doesn't." Harriet flashed a grin, then took another glance up and down the narrow street before passing over a purse to her maid. "You and John Coachman go enjoy the strawberry ices at Gunter's. I shall see you later."

"You're too generous by half, Miss Harriet," murmured Ellie with a reluctant smile. But as the door latch clicked open, a spasm of concern pinched at the corners of her mouth. "Please be careful. All sorts of dangers lurk in this city, and you... well, you are not invincible."

Harriet paused and raised her brows. "Lud, what prompted that?"

"I dunno." Her maid made a face. "Just a queer feeling here." She pressed a hand to her stomach.

A laugh slipped from Harriet's lips. "That's because your breadbox is longing for Gunter's sweets." She quickly descended to the street and made a shooing gesture. "Now be off. And don't fret."

The truth was, danger didn't bother her. Indeed, it seemed to make her feel more... alive.

As the carriage lurched away over the rough cobbles, she drew in a deep breath, savoring the sense of freedom along with the less edifying scents of the surroundings. Modest townhouses lined the perimeter of the square, the crumbling stone and shabby facades a testament that the once-elegant area had seen better days. Her friend, an aging spinster who was working to improve the lot of the poor women in the area, resided in one of the narrow buildings on the far side of the central garden. The two of them had met at a series of lectures on Mary Wollstonecraft's essays, and despite the difference in age had formed a bond over shared intellectual interests. That Lady Catherine possessed an earthy sense of humor and a fascinating—and slightly outrageous—circle of acquaintances made her weekly gatherings for tea and talking about ideas for social reform even more intriguing.

The topic for the upcoming discussion was educational opportunities for girls, and as she hurried through the rusting gate of the square's center garden and cut around the unpruned boxwood hedge to the gravel walkway, Harriet let her mind race over the ideas that had been percolating in her head. Schools ought to teach mathematics and the natural sciences, like astro—

Whomp.

The collision would have knocked her on her derriere, had not a strong pair of male arms arrested her backward fall.

"Charging in where angels should fear to tread?"

Harriet fumbled to straighten the brim of her bonnet, though she didn't need to see the speaker's face to know who it was. Viscount Leete's drawling sarcasm was... unique.

A friend of her older brother since their schoolboy days at Eton, Jack had spent many a term break at her family's home over the years. More recently, they had both played a role in helping his cousin win the hand of Lady Kyra Sterling. As usual, they had engaged in more than their share of verbal sparring. Jack seemed to bring out...

A last tug finally shifted the chip straw bonnet back into place, allowing an unobstructed view of the smirk curled on his handsome mouth. Nettled, Harriet was roused to retort. "Apparently even mere mortals are in peril with the likes of you charging hell for leather around the city."

"*Moi?*" Jack looked down his aristocratic nose. "I was merely walking at a sedate pace. It was you who was barreling along like a bat out of Hades."

Sunlight speared through the windblown tangle of his long hair, setting off a winking of dark and bright, like diamonds dancing over polished ebony. Her breath momentarily seemed to catch in her throat. To clear it, she quickly demanded, "Which begs the question—what are *you* doing here in Red Lion Square?"

"I'm meeting someone," he answered curtly.

A lady, no doubt. And given the environs, likely one of dubious morals, thought Harriet.

"And you?" he added.

"The same."

Jack considered the answer, and for an instant, a mischievous glint lit in his eyes. "One of your radical causes?"

"Yes." That he found it amusing irked her, so she quickly added, "A group of like-minded females is meeting to discuss the inequalities we face in society."

He gave a mock shudder. "I don't know how you do it—I'd rather face a saber-wielding regiment of Death's Head Hussars than have to think that hard!"

The light shifted, and for an instant, it accentuated the dark circles under his eyes and the fine lines of dissipation radiating out from the corners of his mouth.

"So you would rather engage in mindless revelries that will likely kill you just as surely as sharpened steel?"

Jack's jaw hardened, but he remained uncharacteristically silent.

"After being given a second chance at life," she went on, "you ought to take care to make the most of it."

"Thank you for the advice," he said with exaggerated politeness. "I know I can always count on you to be pragmatic and rational."

"Quite right—I'm stick-in-the-mud Harriet." She felt a flush rise to her cheeks. "It seems a lady is damned if she uses her brain and damned if she doesn't."

"I-I didn't mean it as an insult," he muttered.

"Of course you did," she replied tartly. "I'm outspoken and opinionated. Men find that abhorrent."

The last vestiges of mirth gave way to an expression... an

expression she couldn't begin to fathom. "I'm not sure men have the slightest idea of what they want," he said softly.

Harriet was surprised by the note of wistfulness shading the ironic quip. Or perhaps it was only a figment of her own imagination. Either way, it left her feeling unsettled.

"I had better be going, else I'll be late," she said brusquely.

"*Moi aussi,*" he murmured.

Jack was speaking French? Knowing the wartime ordeal he had been through, she wasn't sure whether that boded well or not for his current state of mind. Not that his behavior should be any concern of hers.

Confused, she simply gave a vague wave and turned to continue on to Lady Catherine's townhouse.

"One last thing, Harry…"

She paused and looked back over her shoulder.

"Be careful. This is a dangerous area for you to be out walking on your own."

"You're the second person who has warned me of that today."

His dark lashes shuttered his gaze. "Then perhaps you should pay twice as much attention."

Harriet the hedgehog. Prickly and prone to assume a defensive posture when teased. Unsure whether to laugh or gnash his teeth, Jack watched her stalk away. That was, he supposed, why he couldn't resist the urge to cross verbal swords with her—but only because she could hold her own. Indeed, at times her wit could be even sharper than his.

However, just now it seemed his bantering barbs had slipped under her guard and cut to the quick. *Damnation.* He hadn't meant to hurt her.

But he had.

Injured pride pulsed from the tight set of her shoulders, the stiffness of her gait. Even her skirts seemed to flounce and flutter with anger as she crossed the street.

Expelling a harried sigh, Jack shook off all thoughts of Harriet. He, too, was in danger of being late for a far more important tête-à-tête with a lady from his past.

CHAPTER 2

"*Y*ou came."

"Did you doubt that I would?" Jack slid into the empty seat at the tiny table tucked in the shadows of the coffeehouse.

Camille looked down into her cup. "I—I don't know what to think these days," she said in a low voice. "Or feel."

"Then let me help you sort things out." He leaned forward, quelling the desire to reach out and place a reassuring hand on her cheek. The murky light couldn't hide the familiar shape of her face or the fine-boned features that made her so achingly lovely.

Swallowing hard, he forced his eyes away from the curve of her jaw. "Tell me what's wrong."

"I—I hardly know where to start."

His lips quirked upward for an instant. "In my experience, it's always best to start at the beginning."

"Ah, *oui*. The beginning." She tucked a curl of her honey-colored hair behind her ear. "*Mon Dieu*, that seems like a century ago."

Though a whirl of questions was spinning inside his head, he remained silent, giving her a chance to compose her thoughts.

"And yet, it was only shortly after you left us that disaster struck. Our regiment was retreating with Soult's forces, and Pierre was ordered to hold off the British advance guard while the rest of the army crossed through a treacherous mountain pass." She lifted her coffee cup to her lips but put it down without tasting a drop. "Your troops outnumbered us and forced us to fall back. In the confusion, Pierre was captured."

"Was he injured?" Jack was ashamed of himself for feeling a stirring of hope somewhere deep within the most primitive part of his being.

Camille shook her head. "*Non.* At least that is what we were told. Word came from Soult's staff that he was being taken to England with the other prisoners of rank."

"That is good news," he replied. It was now clear as to why she was in England. "Captured officers give their parole and are allowed to live very comfortably in their assigned town—as long as they keep their word and don't try to escape. It's all very civilized."

"Yes, so I have been told," she murmured.

"As for arranging his release, it shouldn't be difficult to negotiate an exchange of prisoners—"

"But that is the trouble," interrupted Camille. "You see, Pierre seems to have vanished. No one in authority seems to know anything about his whereabouts!"

"Vanished?" Jack frowned. "That's impossible. There are reams of official paperwork kept—"

"*Poof!*" Camille fluttered her graceful hands, her rings setting off a momentary explosion of emerald light against the rough-plastered wall. "The clerks at Horse Guards insist there is no record of his existence."

That made no sense. Unless, of course, her husband had perished during the sea voyage and the report from the Navy had not yet reached the right desk in the warren of government offices...

Again, Jack quelled the ugly little longing stirred by the thought. Pierre had been a friend.

"Alas, *cheri*, the truth is, things have become terribly tangled. You see, it turns out Pierre has influential enemies within the Royalist exiles here in England. They think that he has betrayed his heritage for siding with the Revolution."

"Pierre is an aristocrat?" Jack hadn't been aware of that.

"A minor cadet branch—but yes, he comes from a very old and respected family of the ancient regime." Camille placed her palms on the table and leaned in close—close enough that he could see the tears pearled on her golden lashes. "I'm afraid for him, Jack. And I don't know whom to trust. The diplomats of my own government have warned me to have no contact with the Royalists. Yet I've received a message that the only hope I have of seeing Pierre alive is to negotiate with them."

"So that was who you were meeting with last night."

She nodded.

"What do they want?" asked Jack. "Money? If so, you need not worry. I am a very wealthy man."

"You are too kind, *cheri*. But no, it's not money. Since you ask for the truth..." Her lips quivered. "They know of our connection to you." A pause while she took a deep breath to still the trembling.

"Go on," he urged, when it seemed she might not continue.

"You must understand, I... I never meant to contact you."

"Damnation, Camille." He touched her hand, just for an instant. "We are friends. You must tell me everything."

She hesitated, then expelled a sigh. "They seem to think you might, on account of your connections in the war ministry, know certain information that you would be willing to share with me."

A single teardrop fell as she blinked, and he watched it slowly meander down the soft curve of her cheek before asking, "What sort of information?"

"Nothing really secret. Just a general sense of what the feeling is between England and her allies—who wields the real power, who is bickering with whom, that sort of thing. The Royalists are anxious to play a role in Continental politics if Napoleon should fall, but to do so they need to know... on which side their bread is buttered."

Jack drummed his fingers on the tabletop, suddenly recalling Harriet's earlier angry observation. *Damned if I do, damned if I don't.* For a moment he was disappointed that Camille would suggest such a thing, even obliquely. But then, he reminded himself that he had insisted.

And she was desperate.

"I'm not sure you understand the intricacies of international diplomacy," he replied. "To pass on any sort of information I hear from a well-placed friend, especially to a foreign group, would be a betrayal of confidence at the very least, and perhaps worse."

Her eyes widened at the word 'betrayal'. "Oh, you cannot think I meant to ask you..."

"No," he said gently. "Of course not. But now you understand why, even for you and Pierre, it's not something I could ever contemplate." He shifted in his seat, trying to discern what emotions were rippling in the depths of her hazel eyes. "What I can do is make inquiries with the senior officials at Horse Guards regarding Pierre. I will find him—"

"No. I dare not," she whispered.

"I will be discreet."

"No." The word had an edge of panic to it. "Promise me you won't go to the British authorities."

He drew a measured breath. "Very well. If that is what you wish."

"It is." She looked away. "Indeed, I-I think it best that you simply forget all about meeting me."

"I can't do that," said Jack flatly. "You dragged me back from the dead—you both did. Both my conscience and my sense of honor demand that I not turn my back and walk away."

Camille touched a fleeting caress to the back of his hand, then drew back. "But I am giving you no choice."

There is always an infinite range of choices in life, he thought. The world was rarely painted in stark hues of black and white.

"Where are you staying?" he asked after another few moments of awkward silence.

"I can't tell you that." She expelled a ragged sigh. "The situation is far more complicated than you know, Jack."

He had no illusions about how deeply the tangled web of intrigue was woven into every crack and crevasse of London. Every foreign power had agents spinning plots, and no matter his own feelings on the matter, here on English soil, she would be seen as the enemy.

"At least agree to another meeting with me," he demanded. "You may change your mind about what I have offered." Perhaps it was cruel, but he pressed on. "Or have things changed for you."

Camille paled.

"Tomorrow," he pressed.

"No, the day after," came her reply. "In the evening, rather than the bright light of day." She glanced around nervously before drawing the appointed hour on the table with her finger rather than saying it aloud.

"I'll be here," said Jack. As she rose to take her leave, he added, "And if you're not, I'll assume some misfortune has befallen you and will turn the city inside out to find you."

"I'll be here," she echoed.

Before he could say more, Camille had melted away into the shadows, leaving naught but a faint trace of her perfume.

~

THE DISCUSSION on educational reforms was utterly fascinating, and yet Harriet was having a devil of a time trying to keep her mind from wandering.

"...and that is the list of subjects I would demand that girls be taught," finished her hostess. "Have you any to add, Miss Farnam?"

"Hmm?" She snapped to attention at the sound of her name. "Er, what was that?"

"Lady Catherine asked if you would like to sail to the moon in a spun sugar gondola," answered Miss Breville, a scholarly Bluestocking. Her long, serious face betrayed the hint of a rare smile.

"Pulled by a matched pair of gold and purple unicorns," added Mrs. Griffin. For a minister's wife, she possessed a very whimsical sense of humor as well as strong organizational skills.

"Your thoughts appear to have traveled far past the moon and all the way to Uranus," quipped Lady Catherine. "Might I ask just what has you so preoccupied?"

"Men," admitted Harriett with a huff of disgust.

Mrs. Currough, the notorious Irish Beauty—and London's leading courtesan—gave a knowing nod. "They are, to be sure, difficult creatures, Miss Farnum. You see, dogs and horses may be trained to obey simple commands." She gave a playful wink. "Men are not nearly so clever."

A titter of laughter ran through the room.

"The key is not to fall in love with them."

"I've no intention of falling in love," she assured the Irish Beauty. "Besides, I'm not the sort who would ever inspire a sonnet. I'm outspoken and I'm... unattractive."

"Hmmm." Mrs. Currough tapped at her chin and subjected Harriet to a lengthy scrutiny. "Actually, you're quite wrong. With a different hairstyle, and a gown designed to flaunt your physical assets rather than hiding them under a proverbial bush, you would have men swooning at your feet."

"Ha!" muttered Harriet. "There is an old adage that says one can't make a silk purse out of a sow's ear."

"You might be surprised," countered Mrs. Currough with an enigmatic smile.

Betty McNulty, who in her persona as the flamboyant Madame Deauville ran one of London's most exclusive dress-maker's shops, nodded in agreement. "Colors, textures, what to drape and what to bare—beauty is often a well-crafted illusion."

Harriet frowned. "But—"

"She's right," agreed Lady Catherine. "There are, of course, a few ladies—a *very* few—who are blessed from birth with the looks of a Greek Goddess. But for the rest of us, an artful hand and eye must help augment our natural gifts, such as they are."

"Very true." Mrs. Currough set aside her cup of tea. After cocking her head at several different angles, she said, "Stand up and slowly turn around, Miss Farnum."

"Absolutely not!"

"Oh, go ahead, Harriet," urged Miss Ashmun.

"We are here to discuss serious subjects," she protested. "Not indulge in frivolous fripperies."

"Men and women, and what draws them together, is a *very* serious subject," asserted Mrs. Currough.

Harriet was rarely at a loss for words, but she could think of no rejoinder.

"Come, don't be shy. This will be very educational for all of us," murmured Lady Catherine.

"Very well. I feel like the veriest of fools, but am willing to provide an interlude of amusement for everyone." Shaking out her skirts, she rose from the sofa and self-consciously stepped to the center of the drawing room.

"Head up, shoulders back, spine straight as steel," murmured Mrs. Currough. "No matter how vulnerable you feel, you must always enter a room like you own it."

Harriet gingerly raised her chin.

"Higher," commanded Mrs. Currough. "You may not have been born a princess, but you can act like one."

One of the other ladies present turned to a fresh page in her notebook and surreptitiously jotted down a few lines.

Strangely enough, Harriet did feel slightly regal as she drew herself up to her full height.

"There, you see how the ribcage is elongated, and the bosom presses outward," explained Mrs. Currough. "Every woman looks more elegant, more refined when she isn't afraid to stand tall." She rose and made several slight adjustments to Harriet's posture. "And with the shoulders set back, instead of hunched forward, the arch of the neck is accentuated."

A murmur of assent sounded, followed by more whispers of pencils scribbling on paper.

"Now kindly take a few steps, Miss Farnum."

Harriet did as she was asked.

Mrs. McNulty winced. "You are not carrying coals from Newcastle, dearie. Be a little lighter on your feet. Try to glide, not stomp."

For the next quarter hour, Harriet was poked, prodded and paraded around the room as, much to the edification of the rest of the group, Mrs. Currough shared her expertise on how to appear alluring to men.

"Oh, this has been *very* enlightening," remarked Miss Ashmun. "Er, might we have another session on this topic at the end of next week's meeting?"

The suggestion was greeted with great enthusiasm from the other group members.

"Perhaps Mrs. Currough should think of writing a book on the social graces—The Courtesan's Guide to Capturing a Gentleman's Eye," suggested Lady Catherine with a smile.

"I am happy to reveal my secrets to my friends, but as for a wider audience..." The Irish Beauty let out a low-throated chuckle. "There should remain an air of mystery to what makes a lady alluring, don't you think?"

Be mysterious. Harriet added that nugget of wisdom to the others she had committed to memory. Loath as she was to admit it, the lesson had been very interesting. She had always equated the notion of 'charm' with silly, simpering flirtation, but apparently, it was far more nuanced than that.

As for the physical aspects...

She smoothed at her gown, suddenly aware of the frills and flounces that did little to complement her figure. Perhaps—just perhaps—she would take up Mrs. McNulty's generous offer and pay a visit to Madame Deauville's establishment.

In the meantime, she could practice the advice to "glide, not stomp" later that evening. She had promised her close friend, Lady Theodora Bingham, to accompany her to Lord and Lady Sage's ball. And while neither of them would have any invitations to dance, sharing her new knowledge in the shadowed corner of the room where the informal League of Wallflowers gathered would provide a perfect way to while away the boring hours.

CHAPTER 3

Swearing under his breath, Jack tied off the tails of his cravat with an impatient tug and turned away from the looking glass.

"Damnation," he added in a louder voice. He would much rather spend the evening alone with a bottle of brandy mulling over what he might do to help Camille and her missing husband.

But a promise was a promise, and he had given his word to Anthony Taft, an old friend, that he would make an appearance at the ball Anthony's parents were giving in honor of their daughter's debut into Society.

Apparently, his much-trumpeted return from the dead had made him quite a feather in the cap for any hostess.

Promises, promises.

Jack ran a hand through his hair, undoing the cursory attempt he had made to brush the long locks into order.

Despite his pledge to Camille, he was not about to let her face the dangers and deceptions alone. He would, of course, honor his word, however, there were plenty of ways for him to investigate the mystery of Pierre's disappearance without going to the authorities. After doing his duty for Anthony, he planned to quietly take his leave and head to his club, where he could begin making discreet inquiries.

A short while later, as he joined the crush of guests jostling their way up the grand marble staircase, he was cursing yet again, reminded of how much he disliked the glitter and insincere flatteries of Polite Society. Total strangers were clapping him on the back and mouthing effusive compliments, while those people he knew spouted nonsense about him being a glorious hero.

As if taking a blade of steel to the chest had anything to do with heroism. The truth was, he had merely been too confused and too paralyzed by the mayhem to move.

"Why the black face?" James edged up beside him and offered him one of the two glasses of champagne he had just plucked from the tray of a passing waiter.

"Thank God," muttered Jack as he quaffed a quick swallow of the effervescent wine. "I find these opulent entertainments oppressive. Heaven forbid that people say what they really think."

James let out a wry chuckle. "You mean such things as the Duchess of Deerfield shouldn't be allowed to appear in public wearing a gown which reveals that much quivering flesh?"

Jack choked back a snort. "Perhaps this enforced interlude won't be as bad as I imagined. We can spend the requisite half hour making rude comments about all the other guests."

A mischievous glint sparked in James's eyes. "That," he murmured, "would be evil."

"What are you two devils chortling about?" Their hostess approached and tapped her fan to Jack's shoulder. "Stop conspiring with each other and go dance with the young ladies." A fond smile flitted over her lips, as she had known them since they were mere sprats at Eton. "What good is it to have two of the most eligible rapscallions in London attending my ball if you won't go cause a few swoons?"

"We shall endeavor not to shock the young innocents into a faint," drawled Jack.

"Hmmph." She raised an elegant brow. "How disappointing."

James coughed to cover a laugh.

"And now, I had better go greet the Dragons." She gestured toward a group of turbaned matrons seated by the arrangement of potted plants.

"I suppose we had better go do our gentlemanly duty," muttered James. "I've always found it a good strategy to ask one of the wallflowers to dance, rather than any of the reigning belles, when one is looking to make a quick exit. There's no chance of getting caught up in an endless *pas de deux* of flirtation. One dance, and then after leading her back to the shadows, one can discreetly slip off."

"Excellent," answered Jack. "I'm looking to scamper as well."

"Care to join me at Lucifer's Lair?"

"Perhaps another evening. I've other plans tonight."

James curled a knowing smirk. "Which I suspect involve a lady."

"In a manner of speaking," murmured Jack as they started to make their way to a colonnaded alcove at the far end of the ballroom.

His friend accepted the oblique answer without any further questions. "Speaking of ladies—or rather, ladybirds—I spotted the lovely Mrs. Currough riding in the park this morning. What a stunner." He slanted a glance around the room. "No matter all their august titles and fancy finery, none of the female guests here can hold a candle to her. She has a... a certain presence, though it's bloody hard to define."

"Don't bother trying," advised Jack. "She's under Brentford's protection. Given his fortune and the fact that he's known for being exceedingly generous to his paramours, I doubt she would be tempted to leave."

"Lucky dog," replied James. "Ah, well."

Jack shifted his attention from the jewel-tone swirl of silks and satins on the dance floor to the shadowed recesses up ahead.

There were several small clusters of young ladies huddled together—

His gaze paused on a familiar face. He was surprised to see Harriet here, given her assertions that she found the frivolities of Polite Society a bore. It was a sentiment he shared, but given their uncomfortable encounter earlier in the day, he decided it might be best to avoid another tête-à-tête, no matter that the requisite wallflower dance would be far more interesting with her as a partner. There were few other ladies of his acquaintance who could converse intelligently on such a wide range of subjects. Her experience as a diplomat's daughter...

His steps slowed. Clearing his throat with a brusque cough, Jack glanced at his friend. "Jamie, do me a favor. Do you mind if I claim Miss Farnum, while you take her friend."

"You wish for me to partner the plump one?" asked James.

"She's actually a great gun," said Jack, rising to Theodora Bingham's defense. "Truly." Theo had been a loyal ally in helping his cousin and Kyra Sterling thwart the scoundrel threatening to break up their romance, and he considered her a friend. "It's just that I have something I wish to discuss with Miss Farnum."

"Oh, very well," conceded James. "What does it matter? I simply want to make a few twirls across the parquet and then hare off to more entertaining activities."

They rounded the arrangement of potted palms, and found that Harriet and Theo had moved even deeper into the leafy shadows. The two of them appeared engrossed in a private conversation, and when Harriet looked around, a pinch of annoyance seemed to tug at the corners of her mouth.

"Forgive us for interrupting," began Jack.

"Halloo, Harry," intervened James. "How is William? Is he still in Boston with the Foreign Office's trade delegation."

"Yes, he is. Until springtime." Harriet turned to her friend. "Lord Osborne was also a schoolfriend of my brother. And even more of a scamp than Jack."

Smiling, James inclined an exaggerated bow as Harriet made the formal introductions. "I am charmed to make your acquaintance, Lady Theodora. Might I request the pleasure of the next dance?"

"Y-You wish to s-step out with me?" stammered Theo, a furious blush rising to ridge her cheeks.

"Yes, well, that's rather the idea." James's mouth twitched in amusement. "Dancing does require moving one's feet."

Theo turned even redder.

Feeling a surge of sympathy, Jack shot his friend a warning look that was meant to say *Be Nice To Her*. Theo was engagingly smart and possessed a sharp sense of humor, but until her initial shyness with strangers wore off, she tended to sound like a stuttering schoolgirl.

"Theo floats like a dream over the polished parquet," he assured his friend.

Harriet caught his eye and smiled her thanks.

"Yet another reason I won't take 'no' for an answer." Giving her no chance to protest, James placed Theo's hand on his arm and escorted her out to where the next set was forming on the dance floor.

"James may be an incorrigible scamp, but he is capable of gallantry when he so chooses," observed Harriet.

"Surprisingly enough, he does occasionally rise to the occasion." He held out his arm. "As for me, I claim no such praise for gentlemanly conduct. I have an ulterior motive for asking you to dance."

It was, she knew, foolish to feel a tiny stab of disappointment. Quickly masking her feelings with a cool smile, she took care to match his casual tone. "But of course. Why else?"

A momentary shadow seemed to pass over his eyes, but she

dismissed it as merely the stirring of the palm fronds in a puff of breeze. The musicians struck up first chords of the music as they took up a position on the perimeter of the polished parquet, and Jack guided her through the first few figures of the waltz in silence before answering.

"There are reasons I seek you out other than crass expediency, Harry," he murmured. "You're good company."

"I believe I've just been damned with faint praise."

He chuckled. "You know what I mean."

Unfortunately, I do.

"What is it you wish to ask?" she replied after they had spun through a twirl.

"Your father is involved in the negotiations with our allies on the future of France if Napoleon finally falls, is he not?"

She nodded.

"I'm curious to know whether he has any dealings with the Royalist exiles here in London, and what his opinion is of their leaders."

"He does, and he isn't impressed with any of them. According to him, they are a quarrelsome lot whose jockeying for power is based on personal vanity and greed rather than any real concern for their country."

Jack's expression turned shuttered and for a moment he seemed lost in thought.

"You seem to have a sudden interest in the land of the Frogs," she observed.

"What makes you say that?" he said warily.

"You were mumbling in French earlier today," answered Harriet. Something havey-cavey was definitely afoot, though she had no idea what it was. "But clearly you don't intend to confide the reason as to why."

Another prolonged silence as they moved through an intricate combination of steps. Jack seemed to be doing some mental dancing, too, though judging by the frown tightening on his face, his thoughts seemed increasingly out of tune with the capering notes of the violins.

"I can't," he finally replied. "It isn't my secret to share."

"Very well."

He expelled a harried sigh. "Thank you for that."

"For what?"

"For not pressing me." His mouth compressed to a grim line. "Look, I know I have no right to ask for your help, but if your father would be willing to share any information on the Royalist leaders—who is allied with whom, strengths and weakness in their personalities... that sort of thing—I would be very grateful."

"Anyone in particular?"

He gave her three names.

Harriet thought for a moment. "Are you working for the generals at Horse Guards, or is this personal?"

"Personal," answered Jack after a flicker of hesitation. "Does it matter?"

"Not really," she said. "I am simply curious."

The music was cresting to a crescendo. The couples around them were whirling faster and faster, turning the dance floor into a dizzying blur of colors and the diamond-bright flashes of precious gems.

"Well, will you do it?" he asked.

"We're friends, Jack. And friends help friends, even if the reasons for asking are somewhat murky."

A smile slowly curled on his lips.

No man ought to possess such a sinfully sensuous mouth.

Harriet looked away abruptly, hoping he would dismiss her stumble as mere clumsiness.

"Is it true," she asked abruptly, "that a gentleman likes a lady to be mysterious?"

Jack seemed taken aback by the question. "I hadn't really thought of it in those terms. But yes, I suppose so. A puzzle is a challenge. It begs to be solved."

"Ah." Aware that the music had ended and the other couples were already drifting away, Harriet stopped in mid-step. "Your duty is now done. You can escort me back to the League of Wallflowers and head off to whatever more alluring entertainments you have planned for the night."

JACK WAS STILL PUZZLING over Harriet's odd behavior as he slipped out through the back gardens of the stately townhouse and made his way to the adjoining side street to flag down a passing hackney. Their exchanges usually had the same well-worn fit of a favorite waistcoat. The pattern was familiar—he teased, she bristled—and comfortable.

Tonight had been... different. Something about her seemed altered. If he didn't know better, he would have said she had grown a few inches, for she appeared to take up just a little more of the room.

Frowning, he tried to shake off such addlebrained thoughts. Harry was Harry. If she seemed a little calmer, a little more composed, perhaps it was because she had tippled an extra glass of champagne.

But whatever the mysterious aura surrounding her tonight, he had more pressing conundrums to solve.

The breeze tugged at his coat, and as he stood waiting for a hackney to take him to his club, Jack went over the three names he had mentioned to Harriet, trying to jog his memory for any bit of information he might have read about them in the newspapers.

"Damnation," he muttered, stamping his feet on the pavement to ward off the damp chill blowing in from the river.

"What did Harriet do to cut up your peace?" James joined him on the pavement. "She does have a tongue like a razor at times, and isn't shy about using it."

"Nothing," growled Jack. "Harry has nothing to do with my mood."

"Right-o." His friend clasped his hands behind his back and turned to stare down the opposite end of street.

Jack stomped his feet again, aware of how badly he was behaving with an old friend. "Forgive my ill-humor. Someone I know is in trouble and it is deucedly frustrating that I can't figure out how to help."

James gave a curt nod of sympathy but tactfully remained silent.

After another few brooding moments of contemplating the cracks in the pavement, Jack looked up. "What do you know of the Frogs who gather at Lucifer's Lair?"

"They drink too much and wager too wildly," replied his friend. The moonlight played over the sardonic expression that hardened his handsome features. "Don't we all?"

"Quite likely," agreed Jack. "But aside from the usual debaucheries that take place in a gaming hell like the Lair, what is your impression of the leaders?"

James shrugged. "I have little contact with them. You ought to ask Ingalls. He often plays *vingt-un* with Amirault and his cronies."

A hackney turned down the side street and rumbled to stop.

"You go ahead. I'll wait for another as I'm heading east."

"On second thought," said Jack. "I've changed my mind. I'll come with you."

"FANCY THAT." Her face still a little flushed from dancing, Theo tucked an errant lock of hair behind her ear. "A Wallflower waltzing with the Adonis of Mayfair. I had better pinch myself to make sure I am not dreaming."

"Jamie has more sense than I give him credit for," murmured Harriet.

"I don't think sense had anything to do with it. If you will note, Lord Osborne slipped out through the side salon right after the music finished. I was a tactical advantage, allowing him to escape, nothing more." A faint smile flitted over her face. "Still, it was rather nice to be twirling across the ballroom floor in the arms of a handsome rogue. It's not likely to happen again anytime soon."

"Of course it will," said Harriet absently. She had noted that Jack had disappeared as well and couldn't help but wonder where he had hared off to.

Somewhere French is spoken, she thought a little acidly, then chided herself for being ridiculous. Jack's affairs were of no concern to her.

Or shouldn't be.

"Don't be silly," responded Theo, as if echoing her own inner jeers. "I'm not the sort of lady who will ever capture a gentleman's fancy. I know that." A breathless little sigh escaped her lips. "So it's a moment to be savored."

Shoving her own brooding aside, Harriet turned to her friend. "Capturing a gentleman's fancy has nothing to do with the things you think are important. Beauty and charm come from within."

Theo let out a low snort. "That's the sort of cheery nonsense you hear from your mother or grandmother."

"And yet it's true. I have it from the highest authority on what gentlemen desire," countered Harriett.

A pause. "Who?"

She lowered her voice to a whisper. "Mrs. Currough, the most sought-after courtesan in London."

Theo's eyes widened. "I heard Lady Adelaide Hunter and her sister whispering about Mrs. Currough at Gunter's. The Irish Beauty is said to have every man in Town groveling at her feet."

She glanced around before asking, "Wherever did you, er, encounter her?"

"She attends the meetings on social reform held by Lady Catherine," answered Harriet. "After today's discussion on education for girls, the talk turned to men, and Mrs. Currough was kind enough to share her thoughts on how a lady captivates their attention. She believes beauty is all about the art of illusion."

"How fascinating," mused Theo. "Er... such as?"

Harriet explained what she had heard. "She has promised to continue the lessons at the next meeting. Would you like to come along?"

"My parents would expire on the spot if they heard I was keeping company with a fallen woman—and a notorious one at that."

"You may tell them you are spending the afternoon with me." Harriet paused. "It won't be a lie."

"True." Theo's face scrunched in thought, and the longing light in her eyes showed how much she wanted to cast caution to the wind. "I am not nearly as adventurous as you are, Harry. I don't have the nerve or the imagination."

"Are you trying to convince me or yourself?" asked Harriet softly. "Because if it's me, you are wasting your breath. I know you have courage and boldness in spades."

Theo opened her mouth to speak but Harriet didn't give her a chance. "Look at how resourceful and clever you were in helping Lady Kyra out of a terrible coil. But the trouble is, you see yourself through a different set of spectacles, one whose lenses are distorted by your own expectations."

"I..." Theo drew in a lungful of air—and then let it out in a reluctant laugh. "I am not quite sure whether I've just been complimented or castigated."

"Perhaps a little of both."

They smiled at each other.

"In that case, I would be foolish not to take heed of both exhortations. Mayhap it's time for me to be a bit more daring."

"That's the spirit. I, too, have been thinking the same thing." Harriet freed a palm frond from the ribbons of her upswept hair, suddenly tired of being seen as naught but Harry the Harridan, an outspoken, opinionated Bluestocking. She wanted to be just a little bit exotic and alluring. A little bit mysterious. "It seems that the League of Wallflowers has just resolved to turn over a new leaf."

"Or at least blossoming forth with a few new petals." Theo glanced down at the profusion of pale yellow flounces festooning her bodice and made a face. "I have let Mama take charge of choosing my ballgowns, even though I know she has no eye for fashion. But now I look forward to hearing what Madame Deauville has to say on the subject."

Stepping out from the shadows of the ornamental trees, Harriet boldly signaled to one of the footmen to bring over two glasses of champagne. "Let us toast to—"

"To having men grovel at our feet?" suggested Theo with a mirthful grin.

"I would settle for a sonnet. But even that may be asking too much." She watched the tiny bubbles fizz and froth within the cut-crystal flute. "Let us just raise a glass to following our hearts, wherever they may lead."

CHAPTER 4

Twilight deepened, the hazy rose and gold hues of sunset giving way to the dusky purples presaging the fall of night. From his vantage point under the eaves of an old warehouse, Jack observed the entrance to the tavern, keeping careful watch on the coming and goings. Satisfied that Camille had not been followed, he eased away from the slatted wood and hurried to join her inside.

She was reading a piece of paper, and the single guttering candle in the wall sconce played over her alabaster skin, accentuating the delicate planes of her profile.

Draw in a lungful of air, he reminded himself. Her beauty always seemed to leave him bereft of breath.

She looked up and smiled.

His body seemed unable to obey even the most basic command from his brain. Against all reason, a surge of longing seemed to bubble through his blood.

"Have I come to have freckles on my face?" she asked in a sultry voice.

"There is nothing wrong with freckles," he replied, a sudden vision of Harriet's sun-dappled cheeks popping to mind. Shaking it off, he added, "But no, you are, as usual, the very picture of perfection."

Her smile crooked down at the corners. "You are, as usual, too kind. I look a fright. Your English weather—rain-sun, rain-sun—is very harsh for those of us used to the softer climes of the south."

"Then it would be wise to avail yourself of protection from the elements," Jack said softly.

The candlelight flickered, casting her eyes in shadow. "Come. Sit," replied Camille after darting a look around the taproom. "We ought not to draw attention to ourselves."

Too late for that, he thought as he slid into his chair. Despite the hooded cloak she was wearing, the peek of her profile and glimmer of honey-gold hair was already drawing furtive stares.

"Any news?" he asked.

"Yes." Her voice dropped a notch. "I've received a message—I know not from whom—saying Pierre has been located."

"*Where?*" he asked urgently. "We can now begin to unravel this knot and get him released."

"I... I don't know."

Her slight hesitation stirred a frisson of alarm in the back of his head.

"I was only told it was somewhere in the north."

Jack frowned, his suspicion sharpened by the fact that her gaze slid away from his. His fingers slid across the rough wood and gently clasped her wrist. "Camille, look at me. I sense there is something you are not telling me."

She turned, her eyes shimmering with tears. "I have told you all I know," she insisted. "I have been ordered to be patient, and not to press any inquiries. *Mon Dieu*, can you blame me for appearing frightened and confused?"

Feeling like a bullying brute, Jack released his hold and leaned back. "I'm sorry. It pains me to see you suffering and I want to help."

"I know that, *cheri*. But truly, it would be best if you stay... how do you say it in English... at arm's length from this."

His arms yearned to have her far closer than that. But quelling the ungentlemanly urge to enfold her in a hug, Jack merely gave a gruff nod. "I understand your fears, Camille. But I think you underestimate my powers to help you out of this coil. The Jack Greeley you nursed back to health was a weak, dispirited fellow who had lost the fire in his belly. I'm a different man now."

She was staring at him intently. "Yes, I can see that."

"By some miracle, my cousin also survived the battle. I returned home and found him alive and well at Hendrie Hall."

"That must have been a joyous reunion."

"It was. I felt as though I had been granted a second chance in life."

For an instant, he recalled Harriet's admonition to make the most of that gift and felt an inner twinge of guilt. So far he had been doing precious little with his time, save for drinking and brooding.

"And you shall have a joyous reunion too," he quickly added. "Of that I am sure."

She gave a Gallic shrug. "Life is filled with uncertainties, Jack. Who can tell what the future will bring? For now, I have decided to follow the instructions I've been given."

"But—"

"Please, you must honor my wishes. I have friends here— French friends—who are counseling me on how best to deal with the different factions of the émigré community here in England. Despite all your formidable strengths and your kindness, you cannot understand the intricacies involved. I know you mean well, but one misstep could mean..." She drew a slender finger across her throat. "You have seen what my countrymen are capable of when their passions are aroused."

Jack fought back a protest, knowing her words held some truth. But there were also dangers involved in letting her try to navigate the swirling currents and rip tides of Royalist politics on her own.

"Camille, it appears we could argue until Doomsday and not agree on what is the best way to solve this conundrum. At least agree to meet with me regularly, so that I may be assured you are well."

She bit her lip, and her eyes darted to the folded paper by her reticule before meeting his. "For the moment, I will agree. But I cannot promise that won't change."

"I understand." Yes, much could happen to change things, including his own clandestine inquiries into Pierre's disappearance. There had to be some clues, some trail to follow. A French officer couldn't just vanish into thin air.

"Would that you did," she whispered cryptically.

"Camille..." he murmured again, though he wasn't sure what he wanted to say.

She reached out and touched a finger to his lips, the quicksilver gesture happening so fast that a part of him wondered if he had just imagined it. "Don't ask for more than I can give right now, *cheri*. As for the future... who can say what will happen."

HARRIET ARRIVED EARLY at Gunter's Tea Shop for her appointed rendezvous with Theo and found a free table by one of the large windows looking out onto Berkeley Square. Nearly a week had passed since the ball, and her friend was in a flutter of nervous anticipation about coming along on the morrow to the meeting at Lady Catherine's townhouse.

Her lips quirked as she ordered a pot of gunpowder tea. *What sort of sparks am I setting off in Theo's normally placid temperament?* It was all very well to risk stirring up nasty gossip regarding her own actions. She was used to being different from other young ladies, and didn't mind being considered eccentric by the *ton*. But

Theo came from a more conventional household. She was having second thoughts about encouraging her friend to risk clouding her reputation.

Society did not easily forget or forgive.

"Sorry to be late." Theo sat down, sounding a bit breathless from walking with unladylike haste. "I stopped at Hatchards to purchase a book." Her reticule thunked against the marble tabletop. "Several books, in fact."

"Novels or illustrated volumes on garden design?" asked Harriet. Both were great favorites with her friend.

"Neither," replied Theo. "I realized that although you have told me much about Mrs. Wollstonecraft's ideas on the rights of women, I had never actually read her writings. So I found a copy of her *A Vindication on the Rights of Woman*."

Harriet eyed the bulging bag. "And?"

"And a work by John Locke on education reform." A pause. "And the new novel everyone is talking about—*Pride and Prejudice*."

"I fear I'm a pernicious influence on you." She smiled. "If your parents spot those in your possession, they will likely forbid you to see me."

"I do have a mind of my own, Harry," responded Theo quietly. "I may not be as outspoken as you are on certain subjects, but I think about the things you say, and form my own ideas and opinions—not all of which agree with your point of view."

Stunned, Harriet felt her shoulders slump. Was that how her friend saw her—as a vain, pompous prig, puffed up with the conceit of her own self-importance?

"If I've given you the impression that I have anything less than the highest respect for your intellect or opinions, then I've expressed myself very badly," she said in a half-whisper. "And for that I am heartily ashamed. Please accept my apologies."

Theo's flushed face turned even pinker. "No, no, you've no

need for recriminations. If anyone is at fault, it is I. I should be more forceful in expressing my thoughts and feelings."

"This sounds like a very intriguing conversion." James had come up behind them. "Do you mind if I continue to eavesdrop?"

"Yes," responded Theo in a surprisingly strong-willed voice. "As a matter of fact, we do."

James ignored her. Turning to Harriet he asked, "What subject it is that you ladies wish to be forceful about?"

"The new novel, *Pride and Prejudice*," she answered quickly. "Have you read it?"

"As a matter of fact, I have," replied James.

"What did you think of it?" challenged Theo.

Well, well, thought Harriet. Her friend seemed to have lost no time in putting her new resolve into action.

"I enjoyed it very much," he answered. "The author is sharply observant and captures human foibles with excruciating accuracy."

"You seem a trifle surprised that a lady is capable of such perception," murmured Harriet.

"Not at all," assured James with a lazy grin. "I have three sisters. I have long ago learned not to underestimate the capabilities of the female mind."

Theo opened her mouth as if to speak, then shut it.

"And you, Lady Theo?" His attention once again shifted to her friend. "What is your opinion of the story?"

"I—I have not yet read it," she answered reluctantly.

"I look forward to hearing your reaction." A pause as his lips twitched. "Expressed as forcefully as you wish."

Theo's eyes narrowed and a scowl pinched on her face.

A scowl? Theo never scowled. She was good-natured to a fault... Stirring thoughtfully at her tea, Harriet looked up through her lashes and waited.

But before any further sparks could fly, a young lady of perhaps sixteen, rushed up and took James by the arm. "Jamie,

Louisa and I have chosen our ices, and you did promise to pay—"

"No need for shouts and swoons, Georgie. The waiter will not snatch them back and feed them to the pigeons if I am a moment or two late in opening my purse."

The young lady flushed. "I am *not* shouting," she said in a deliberately low voice. "And I've never swooned in my life."

James raised a brow. "You did when I put a frog in your bed."

"I was nine. And it wasn't precisely a swoon."

He chuckled, then gestured at Harriet and Theo. "Allow me to introduce you to my friends, so they won't think you're a hopeless hoyden." To them, he added, "My youngest sister, Georgianna. And despite the evidence to the contrary, she *is* capable of ladylike manners when she so chooses."

"Beast." Georgianna's flush deepened as she turned to Harriet and Theo. "Oh, please do forgive me. But my brother can be—"

"Irritating in the extreme?" suggested Theo.

The young lady expelled an aggrieved huff. "Yes! Precisely."

James laughed again, and performed the introductions.

Georgianna responded with polished poise, earning a wink from her brother. She shot him an aggrieved look before drawing a deep breath and then ventured to add, "I heard you speak at the Horticulture Society on the subject of climbing roses, Lady Theo. Your watercolor sketches were absolutely delightful. I-I wish I could paint half so well."

"Why, um..." Theo looked flustered. "They are only rough dabbles. It is my good friend, Lady Kyra Sterling—now Mrs. Greeley—who is the real artist."

"Lady Kyra is prodigiously talented," intervened Harriet. "But so are you."

James was regarding all of them with an enigmatic look.

"Indeed," agreed Georgianna. "You have a wonderfully whimsical quality to—"

"Your strawberry ice is likely melting," pointed out her

brother. "And we ought to leave the ladies to enjoy their own treats."

Looking horribly embarrassed, Georgianna quickly apologized, but Theo quickly put her at ease by asking if she was going to attend the upcoming Society lecture and, on hearing the affirmative, inviting the young lady to sit with her.

"That was kind of you," murmured Harriet as the two of them returned to their waiting sister.

"Lord Osborne was teasing her unmercifully."

"Brothers do that."

Theo flashed a rueful smile. "Yes, I suppose they do, don't they?" Her gaze seemed to lock on some distant point outside the window. "Rumor has it he is an unrepentant rake."

There was an odd note to her friend's voice that she hadn't heard before.

"All handsome young men are wont to sow their wild oats," replied Harriet after a moment of thought. "I'm not sure whether that makes them unrepentant rakes. We both know that rumor can be much exaggerated. Only look at the ugly things that were said about Kyra."

Theo nodded, but she still looked a little troubled.

"And Jack—some of the whispers floating through the drawing rooms would make your hair curl." On recalling the one she had heard just this morning, which involved a voluptuous ladybird and an ornate fountain on Half Moon Street, she felt an unaccountable tightness take hold of her throat. A quick sip of tea did nothing to help—the brew suddenly tasted bitter.

Knowing her friend's fondness for sweets, Harriet set down her cup and turned her gaze to the display case of pastries. "The almond tart looks divine," she observed, looking to cheer them both up. "Shall we each order a slice?"

Theo hesitated, then shook her head. "You go ahead. I think I shall just have tea."

"Are you feeling ill?"

"No. It's just that I was thinking about what you told me concerning Mrs. Currough and her notions of beauty being all about the art of illusion. If she's right and fabrics can be draped and shirred to trick the eye, it might be wise to give a dressmaker a little less of me to hide."

Theo seemed to be taking the idea of the League of Wallflowers turning over a new leaf quite literally.

As if reading her thoughts, Theo made a wry grimace. "I know it's silly to think anyone, even a fairie sorcerer, can turn a sow's ear into a silk purse."

"You're not a sow's ear, Theo. You're a vibrant, smart young lady who glows with vitality. That is *real* beauty. Why, Jack said as much at the Duke of Pierpont's ball."

"The lens of friendship distorts the view. I am also plain and stout, and that is what most people see." She quirked a smile. "Not that I mind being a wallflower. But occasionally, it would be nice to be asked to dance by a dashing gentleman."

"But you danced with Lord Osborne."

"Yes, I know," came the cryptic answer.

Harriet decided not to try to delve deeper into her friend's odd mood. Her own was confusing enough. Instead, she ordered two fresh pots of tea from a passing waiter, and resolved to put all disquieting thoughts of handsome gentlemen out of her head.

"Speaking of fashion," she said. "You will very much enjoy meeting Mrs. McNulty tomorrow. She's not at all high in the instep, and has a very earthy sense of humor."

"It is hard to imagine that the celebrated Madame Deauville, London's most elite modiste, actually hails from the rookeries of Seven Dials."

"Illusion," murmured Harriet.

Unfortunately, the tall, lean figure who entered the tea shop at that moment was all too real.

So much for banishing men from my mind.

"Ah, there you are, Harry." Jack gave a friendly nod to Theo and pulled up a chair to join them. "I was hoping you hadn't left yet."

"How did you know I was here?" she inquired.

"There is no great mystery to it—I saw your maid on Bond Street."

Would that she could unknot all the mysteries plaguing her thoughts. Beginning with why, at the sight of him, her heart gave a strange little skip and thudded up against her ribs.

"Is something ailing you?"

Her gaze jerked up to meet his teasing smile.

"I thought all ladies adored sweets. Yet here you are, in a place renowned for its sublime confections and the two of you are having naught but tea."

"Mayhap," said Theo quickly, "it's because we are still recovering from indulging in far too many of your cousin's delectable chocolate treats."

"Had I realized chocolate was such a seductively sweet temptation for the opposite sex, I would have offered to serve as his apprentice in the kitchens."

"I have a feeling you have no need to sharpen your skills with the ladies," said Harriet tartly. "Was there a reason you were looking for me—other than to discuss cooking?"

Jack raised a brow at her tone, but his response was merely a curt nod. "Yes," he replied, his playful grin giving way to a more serious expression. "I was..."

His voice trailed off abruptly as his gaze seemed to lock on some spot at the far end of the room.

She waited, but the silence stretched out for another few moments.

"Never mind," he muttered.

Harriet leaned back in her seat, just enough to dart a sidelong glance and catch sight of James approaching, accompanied by his two sisters and a gentleman she didn't recognize.

"Ladies, Louisa insisted on being introduced to you. I hope

you don't mind." He nodded at Jack. "You have had the misfortune of knowing her since she was in leading strings."

Louisa's cheeks turned flame red as she let out a little huff of outrage. "I swear it wasn't me who set the tails of His Lordship's coat on fire."

"However," continued James. "I don't believe you're acquainted with Comte Amirault."

Harriet pricked up her ears. Amirault—one of the three Royalist names Jack had given to her.

As James made the round of introductions, she was quite sure she saw a subtle signal pass between him and Jack when their eyes momentarily met.

Yet another mystery.

She had also caught the dismissive look on Amirault 's face when his gaze flicked over her and Theo. The Frenchman clearly had no interest in two plain-as-biscuits ladies. However, at the mention of her name, his expression quickly changed.

"How delightful to make your acquaintance, Miss Farnum." With a Gallic flourish, he inclined a bow. "Perchance is your father the distinguished diplomat, Sir William Farnum?"

"Yes," replied Harriet coolly, giving a pointed look at Theo.

The Frenchman turned to Jack. "And what an honor to meet one of England's brave war heroes."

Jack murmured a polite reply.

Some sort of intrigue was clearly afoot. If there was one thing Jack abhorred, it was toadeaters.

While she was momentarily distracted by such thoughts, it was James who took note of Theo sitting calmly through the flurry of compliments, betraying no dismay at being totally ignored.

"Indeed, this is quite an illustrious trio," he announced. "Lady Theo is an accomplished artist. Her paintings of roses are much admired here in London."

Harriet shot him a grateful look while Amirault made a perfunctory show of greeting her friend.

After a few more exchanges of pleasantries, James took his sisters in hand. "I see Aunt Imogen's carriage across the square, and you know how cross she gets if you keep her waiting."

The young ladies both made a face.

"Lord Osborne has kindly invited me to join him for a glass of port at White's after he has delivered his charming sisters to their relative," said Amirault. "Might we tempt you to join us, Lord Leete? I should very much like to hear your views on how the war is progressing on the Peninsular."

Jack quickly rose. "Something more potent than tea would be very welcome."

"Excellent," exclaimed the Frenchman.

It wasn't until the group had moved out onto the pavement that Harriet noted a small scrap of folded paper beneath Jack's chair.

"What is that?" asked Theo as she leaned down to retrieve it.

"I don't know." The paper crackled invitingly between her fingers. "It could be anything—a bill from his wine merchant, a list of wagers to make on the upcoming races at Newmarket..." She hesitated. "A billet doux from some secret paramour."

"Or it may not even belong to Jack at all," said Theo reasonably. "Perhaps you should open it, so you know whether it's important to return it."

"Perhaps you are right."

CHAPTER 5

The swish of skirts suddenly rose above the ruffling of the leaves.

"Jack!"

He turned to see Harriet quickening her steps to catch up with him and his two companions as they cut through the square's center gardens.

"Might I have a word with you?" she called.

"You go on," he said to James and Amirault. "I'll catch up with you in a moment."

Seeing him halt, Harriet slowed to a more measured pace. Through the dappled shadows it was impossible to read her expression—a fact that caused his brow to furrow in consternation. *Damnation, her thoughts are usually writ plain on her face.* But of late, since her odd question concerning mystery, they had been difficult to decipher.

As if intent on teasing him into a black humor, she paused when she reached him and took a moment to catch her breath instead of speaking her mind.

"Well?" he asked impatiently. "What is so deucedly important that you had to chase after me?"

Her chin took a defiant jut, a sure sign that she, too, wasn't in the best of moods. "This."

Jack eyed the folded piece of paper she held up and swore silently.

"It must have fallen out of your pocket, for it was under the chair."

"Thank you," he replied curtly, taking it from her outstretched hand.

Harriet responded by telling him he was quite welcome. In French.

"Harry," he began.

"You don't have to say anything more," she interjected. "I didn't have an opportunity to mention it in Gunter's, but I also wanted to tell you that I had a chance to speak to my father about the three names you gave me. There are some things that might interest you, including several nuggets of information on your new friend, Comte Amirault. I've written them up, but as I didn't expect to meet you, I didn't bring them along."

He shifted his stance. "Thank you." She deserved a more appreciative response than that, but he couldn't seem to think of what to say. "Might I stop by your townhouse in the morning to pick them up?"

"Of course." Silk rustled against the smooth gravel. "Don't let me keep you any longer from your port."

"Harry—"

The sounds ceased.

"I don't suppose you are attending Lady Mifflin's musicale tonight?"

"As a matter of fact, I am. Her daughter is a friend. We are both members of the League of Wallflowers."

"The League of Wallflowers?" he repeated. "I thought you didn't give a fig for gardening."

A faint smile played on her lips. "That's what we call ourselves —the unremarkable blooms who cluster together in the dark alcoves at the back of the ballroom. Men prefer the showier specimens, but we've come to greatly enjoy each other's company."

Harriet thinks of herself as unremarkable? Granted, she was not a reigning Diamond of the First Stare, but now that he thought on it, she was quite attractive in her own way.

A low cough roused him from his momentary reverie. Wrenching his gaze up from the intriguing glimpse of creamy flesh exposed by the shallow "v" of her bodice, Jack cleared his throat.

"I enjoy your company, too," he muttered.

Her smile grew more pronounced. "Yes, well, who else would tolerate your infernal teasing?"

"There is that." *And the fact that you're clever and funny.*

"I'll bring the list tonight," she said dryly. "And no need to say 'thank you' again."

He grinned, glad to be back to the usual good-natured banter with her. "Nonetheless, thank you."

As the aria warbled to an end, Theo let out a relieved sigh and whispered, "Annabel possesses a great many laudable talents. Singing is not one of them."

Harriet nodded and waited as the guests seated close by rose and hurried off to the supper room, where a sumptuous array of delicacies were being offered as refreshments. "Unfortunately her mother insists on the lessons, saying a gentleman expects his future wife to have mastered the genteel arts of sewing, singing and sketching."

"There is another activity that begins in 's'," murmured Theo.

Harriet choked down a burble of laughter. "The existence of which no young lady is supposed to admit to knowing, much less mentioning it aloud."

"It seems very strange, doesn't it?" mused Theo. "The thought of it must never cross a young lady's mind, and yet it seems that a young gentleman is encouraged to think of nothing else."

"I hadn't considered it like that, but you are right." She sighed. "Like many of society's strictures, there are two sets of rules. It's very unfair."

"I know it's wrong, but I can't help wondering about it," said her friend in a small voice. "I mean, if men seem to find it so... pleasurable, then it must not be so onerous."

Harriet had experienced far more of the world than Theo, and had come to much the same conclusion. "From what I have seen and heard in my travels, I think you are right. But... but I don't know for sure."

"Neither do I." Theo echoed her sigh. "And perhaps I never will."

They exchanged pensive looks, and then suddenly Harriet let out a laugh. "That is why we need social reform. So we ladies are permitted to know more about life than we do at present."

Theo allowed an impish grin. "Perhaps I'll join Lady Catherine's group for more than just the advice on fashion."

"I think you would find it very—" The sound of someone approaching caused Harriet to cut short her reply.

"Surely you two lovely ladies are growing thirsty with all that talking."

The silky French accent stirred an unpleasant prickling down the length of her spine.

"Allow me to escort you to where they are serving refreshments," continued Amirault. "The lobster patties are *magnifique* and the champagne is excellent."

Harriet reluctantly accepted his hand and rose. Theo was slow to follow, which earned her an irritated glare.

"Do you like music, Comte?" asked Harriet, quelling another little frisson of dislike. Having lived in the carefully choreographed world of diplomacy, she could, when she so chose, mask her true feelings with a show of politeness.

"Not particularly." He winked. "I come for the engaging company and excellent wine. But please don't betray my secrets."

She said nothing in reply.

"*Alors*, may I fetch you a plate of delicacies?" he asked as they passed into the supper room.

"How kind of you. Theo prefers lobster while I am very fond of duck pate," she replied. "We will wait for you by the terrace doors."

"Oh, that was evil of you," whispered Theo as he stalked away.

"His Gallic charm is too oily by half. You saw him when he first met us—we were of no more interest to him than a speck of paint on the wall until he heard that my father was a diplomat." She watched him move through the line at the banquet tables, oozing smiles and polite flatteries. "He's trying to grease the wheels of my vanity because he wants something from me."

Theo considered her words. "Some might call that cynical," she said softly.

"And others would say it's simply realistic." Her gaze strayed back to the crowded room, slowly sweeping over the guests in search of a carelessly combed shock of dark hair. "You prefer to think the best of people, while I prefer to think the worst." With an inward wince, she chided herself for acting like a moonstruck schoolroom chit. If Jack did indeed make an appearance, it was only for the pragmatic reason of fetching her notes on the Royalists.

"That way," she added, "I am rarely disappointed."

On that note, Amirault returned and escorted them to one of the small dining tables set along the perimeter of the room.

They were quickly joined by another Frenchman, whose fair hair and sunny countenance were in sharp contrast to the dark locks and false smile of his countryman.

"Come, Amirault, you must not be allowed to keep these young ladies all to yourself."

The comte did not look happy to see the fellow—which

Harriet decided was a mark in the stranger's favor. Looking up with a smile, she quickly invited him to join them.

"*Merci!*" He inclined a friendly bow. "Permit me to introduce myself—or is that a *faux pas* in English society? I am constantly confusing all your many rules."

"Let us not stand on ceremony, sir. This is an informal gathering, so we may bend the rules a bit," said Harriet.

"Your kindness to a stranger is much appreciated, mademoiselle, I am Alphonse de Beaumont."

Harriet knew his charm was likely as well-practiced as that of Amirault, but it had a more playful ring. She made the requisite responses, and patted the seat beside her.

"Have you been in England long?" she inquired.

"Alas, too long," he replied mournfully. "My family managed to escape the Terror, and we went to live with relatives in America. But two years ago, I chose to come back to Europe, in hopes of helping to restore the monarchy to France."

"It must be hard, being an outcast from your home and your heritage," observed Theo.

Beaumont flashed a sad smile. "*Oui.* But there is a glimmer of hope, now that your General Wellington is beating Bonaparte's armies in the Peninsula."

"The Little Corsican's throne is close to toppling," growled Amirault. "And when it does, order will finally be restored to France."

"Ah, but the question is *whose* order," murmured Beaufort.

So, the two men are at odds? Harriet made careful note of that.

"By the grace of God, it won't be one espoused by you and your misguided leader," snapped Amirault.

Beaumont raised a golden brow. "Are you saying God favors your cause above all others? I, for one, wouldn't dare to presume I have direct contact with Heaven."

Harriet bit back a smile.

"Yet you presume to mock the *ancien regime* and all the past centuries of its noble achievements," retorted Amirault.

"The world is changing. One must change with it."

"Bah!" Amirault lapsed into a sullen silence for several moments, then once again resumed an air of smug superiority. "Don't bore the ladies with talk of politics. I'm sure they would much prefer to discuss far more pleasant things."

"Like the weather?" suggested Harriet.

A glint of amusement lit in Beaumont's hazel eyes.

Amirault, however, was oblivious to the subtle note of sarcasm. Shooting a triumphant smile at his adversary, he said, "It has been unusually nice for this time of year, has it not?"

He kept up a flow of tedious platitudes, until finally, her plate empty, Harriet set aside her fork and made to rise. "Thank you for your company, but I think Lady Theo and I should—"

"Head into the drawing room," finished Amirault smoothly. "Our hostess has arranged for some informal dancing, and knowing how you ladies like to cut a caper, I should be happy to twirl you through the first gavotte."

Harriet was too surprised to evade his hand.

Darting a nasty look at his countryman, he added, "Beaumont shall be delighted to partner Lady Thalia."

To his credit, Beaumont rose and announced quite clearly, "Indeed I would, Lady *Theo*. Would you do me the honor?"

Deciding not to make a scene, Harriet submitted to being escorted to where a swath of carpet had been rolled up to make room for dancing. As the quartet of violins struck up a lively country tune, she spun through the figures, wondering why Amirault had insisted on making a cake of himself. He did not caper well.

Her question was soon answered. At the first pause in the music, as the couples on the dance floor moved to reform the set, he drew her aside and into a paneled alcove displaying a selection of engravings on the flora and fauna of England.

Candles flickered in the wall sconces, painting soft swirls of light over the dark wood. A breeze drifting in through the open leaded glass window tempered the heat of the crowded drawing room. It might have been a pleasant spot... save for the company.

"I must confess, I had not expected to enjoy this evening, but your company has made it most pleasurable, Mademoiselle Farnum."

"Is that so?"

"Very much so." His false smile stretched wider, showing a peek of pearly teeth, and for an instant, he looked just like the print of a weasel hanging by his head—a sly predator that relied on stealth and cunning to capture its prey.

Curious as to what he wanted from her, she replied, "Naturally I'm flattered."

"I have a feeling you understand the world far better than most young ladies, given your father's position as a diplomat." Assuming a mournful expression, he looked up at her through his dark fringe of lashes. "*Alors*, mademoiselle, I miss conversing with someone who possesses both beauty and an appreciation of the role governments play in keeping society safe from chaos."

In other words, you wish to pump me for information concerning what negotiations Britain is making with its allies.

Her first reaction was to throw his recent words about ladies and politics back in his face. But the murmur of French reminded her of Jack's mysterious investigation and the fact that Amirault's name had been of interest to him.

Harriet drew in a measured breath. That there had been another name mentioned in the note she had found under his chair that afternoon also pricked at her memory. *Camille.* She couldn't help but wonder who the lady was and why Jack was so afire to help her vanquish some shadowy threat.

Exhaling a breathy sigh, she with her own false flattery. "Why, Comte Amirault, it is heartening to hear you understand the important role men like my father play in keeping order in these turbulent times."

"Oh, be assured I have the utmost regard for your esteemed Papa." He angled his face into the candlelight, no doubt knowing that his finely chiseled features would make many young ladies go a little weak in the knees. "I hope you will permit me to further our acquaintance so that we may discuss such topics of mutual interest."

Cat and mouse. Harriet gave an inward smile. Let Amirault think he was the one possessing cunning and claws.

"I would like that," she said demurely. "And now, if you will excuse me, the rules of Polite Society dictate that I ought to return to the other guests." A smile. "And a lady must be very careful about not breaking the rules."

CHAPTER 6

A frown formed between Jack's brows as he ran his gaze over the supper room for the second time. Harriet had said she would be here, and unlike so many flighty females, she could always be counted on to do what she said she would.

So where the devil is she?

The notes of a country reel drifted out from the adjoining drawing room, giving some hint as to the answer. Circling around the refreshment tables, he was heading to the doorway when a stout matron, her billowing gown flapping like the topgallants of a ship of the line, sailed in to block his way.

"Lord Leete! How wonderful to see you! Why, the news of your return to England was nothing short of miraculous. I am in alt that you survived. Everyone in Town is."

"Thank you, Lady Keating," replied Jack, trying to edge sideways to slip around her considerable bulk.

She moved with surprising dexterity. "I believe you know my daughters."

It was only now that he noticed she had two young ladies in tow.

"Arabella, Margaret, make your curtsies to the London's most valiant hero," commanded their mother before he could respond.

Gritting his teeth, Jack greeted the giggling pair.

"I vow, you are the talk of the *ton*, sir." Lady Keating winked. "The words on everyone's lips are handsome and heroic. Isn't that true, girls?"

More likely, the words were rich, titled, and available. Over the past few months he had come to feel some sympathy for a fox being pursued by a pack of hounds. Mamas with unwed daughters were even more relentless when it came to running an eligible husband to ground.

More giggles sounded from the young ladies.

Hell's teeth, how he hated the schoolgirl simperings of the misses on the Marriage Mart. After the searing intensity of wartime—the joys, the fears, the horrors—their conversation seemed so supremely silly. He knew it wasn't their fault, and yet...

"La, you must promise to attend my ball next week!" went on Lady Keating. "I shall be sure to have the first waltz played in your honor."

"How kind," he responded, adding a few more polite platitudes while sliding toward the gap between two brocade armchairs. "And now, if you will excuse me..."

This time he managed to outmaneuver her and hurried on his way. Ignoring two other greetings, Jack ducked through the archway and paused in the recessed shadows to draw a steadying breath.

"Damnation," he muttered, feeling a beading of sweat form under his starched evening shirt and trickle over the saber scar on his chest. Wise and worldly, Camille understood the vicissitudes of life. While here in England, most well-bred females were swathed in cotton wool and tucked away in a silk-covered pasteboxes. God forbid that any knock or jostle should mar their porcelain perfection.

Through the swirl of dancing couples, he spotted a flutter of mauve silk at the far end of the room, causing the pent-up air in his lungs to release in a sigh of relief.

And then there was Harriet. A unique force unto herself.

A moment later another figure came out of the same alcove where she had been, and after a glance around, sauntered off to one of the side salons.

Jack slipped out of his refuge and made his way around the perimeter of the room to the set of glass-paned doors leading out to the terrace. Harriet had found a nook between a pair decorative marble columns, and was leaning up against the smooth stone, a pensive look on her face.

"By Jove, I've been looking all over for you. What were you doing with Amirault?" he asked without preamble.

Lost in thought, Harriet must not have heard his approach, for she appeared startled by his words. Now that he was closer, he saw two hot spots of color darkening her cheekbones.

"Dancing," she replied, fanning her flushed face. "And talking."

"About what?"

"It's warm in here. I think I need a breath of fresh air."

Taking the hint, Jack offered his arm and led her out into the cool evening air. Torchieres were set along the stone balustrades, the curling flames undulating in time with the muffled music.

"Amirault is a pompous popinjay—" he began.

"Give me some credit, Jack. I do use my head for something other than a perch for my bonnet."

"Then why—"

"Because there were several things my father mentioned that I wished to verify for myself."

Their steps had brought them to the corner farthest from the doorway. Jack turned to shield her from the breeze blowing in from the garden.

"And did you?"

Light and dark played hide and seek between their bodies. The slope of his shoulders threw her half in shadow. Her eyes were hidden—only a silvery spangle of moonlight glimmered along the curl of her lashes.

For a long moment there was only the faint hiss and crackle of the burning lamp oil. She shifted, and the red-gold fire caught the contours of her profile. It took him several heartbeats before he realized she had started to speak.

"Yes. To begin with, Amirault is not merely a pompous popinjay, he's a pompous ass. But perhaps a dangerous ass if one happens to care about the future of France."

Jack tensed. "What do you mean?"

In answer, papers crackled as she reached into her reticule and pulled out a sheaf of papers. "I've written down all the information here, along with some facts on the other two men you mentioned. My father was in a chatty mood, and the émigré factions have been making delicate negotiations with the heir to the French throne even more difficult with all their squabbling."

Jack carefully tucked the notes into his pocket.

"It seems Amirault's name has been linked with the death of a rival leader, who supposedly was slain during a scuffle with footpads in Green Park. The authorities can't prove foul play, but let's just say the circumstances were suspicious." She went on to give a more detailed report of the information.

"That is exceedingly helpful," he murmured when she finished. Lapsing into thought about what he had just heard, he took her by the arm and began to pace along the length of the railing.

It took several turns to rouse him from his brooding. "You're a real brick, Harry."

"Ah." Jack felt her muscles stiffen. "Mud mixed with water and baked to a dull red finish. How edifying to hear that's the image I bring to mind."

He stared at her, nonplussed. "What's wrong with a brick? It's solid, steadfast, reliable."

She held his gaze for a heartbeat, and then in a very un-Harriet way, she dropped her eyes. "Hardly the qualities that inspire odes of undying passion."

"Confound it, Harry, you don't like that gushingly silly sort of poetry."

A strange flicker seemed to stir beneath her downcast lashes. "*Do* you?"

Her silence made him feel even more flustered. "Hell's bells, I meant it as a compliment."

At that, she looked up with a wry smile. "I know better than to expect compliments from you, Jack."

"Have you imbibed too much champagne?"

"Do I sound intoxicated?"

"No," he admitted. "Just... deucedly odd."

"Mayhap it's something in the night breeze and quicksilver moonlight," responded Harriet. "We should go back inside."

He held his ground. Something seemed different about her, but like the flitting shapes and shadows moving in the mist-shrouded gardens, it remained too elusive to define.

"You're angry."

Harriet lifted her chin a notch. "Not at all. Though perhaps a little nettled that you won't tell me what this is about. If I knew, I could be of more help."

Try to explain about Camille and why he felt compelled to come to her aid? Impossible, as his own feelings were too tangled for him to make any sense of them. Instead, he merely gave a gruff laugh. "I don't need your help. And besides, as you said yourself, these fellows are likely smarmy scoundrels. I don't want you involved with them."

"Because it might be dangerous?"

He recognized the ominous undertone in her voice but hoped

to defuse it by pretending he didn't notice. "Precisely. You've given me all I need to know from your sources. Rest assured there's nothing more for you to do."

"So, I should just go back to my embroidery."

Jack had sinking suspicion that whatever he said, her needle would lance through his tongue. Deciding silence was the best strategy, he turned for the doors.

They walked on for a few steps, and then he suddenly came to an abrupt halt.

"I have it," he muttered.

Her brows arched up in question.

"What's different about you," Jack explained. "I couldn't put a finger on it earlier, but now..." He regarded her quizzically. "You've been gliding like a swan over these stones. And I could swear you've grown an inch or two." His mouth thinned in consternation. "How is that possible?"

"You must be imagining it," replied Harriet softly.

Quite likely. His mind seemed to be whirling in strange circles of late.

As they passed through the portal, Jack hesitated. "You are sure you're not cross as crabs with me? I... I don't like the idea of us being at odds with each other."

"Oh, come. We are always at odds with each other, Jack. That's the reason you seek out my company."

"It's not the only reason," he protested, though if she challenged him to explain it, he would have a deucedly hard time finding the words.

She flashed an enigmatic smile but said nothing in reply. Slipping her gloved hand free from the crook of his arm, she edged away to make a prolonged survey of the drawing room. "I had better go find Theo. She tends to be overcome by shyness in such a crush as this, and I fear she may be cowering in some shadowed corner by herself."

With that, she glided off.

Like a swan, thought Jack. *Most definitely a swan.*

HARRIET KEPT the corners of her mouth curled up until she was sure the crowd had closed around her, a shield of silks and starched linen as carefully arranged as her own features. He mustn't ever guess how much his casual comment had hurt. Would that her flesh was as hard and unfeeling as brick. Impervious to the pain of knowing that to him she was akin to an old pair of riding boots or a well-worn waistcoat—something so familiar and comfortable that he didn't really notice it was there.

Oh, but she noticed *him.* Every chiseled nuance of his face, every subtle contour of his muscled shoulders. The way the light danced through his dark hair, the way the scent of his shaving soap melded with the earthy masculine essence of his skin.

Fool. Harriet closed her eyes for an instant, determined to hold back the tears welling up from within. She prided herself on possessing a modicum of intelligence. And allowing a *tendre* for a handsome, devil-may-care rogue to take hold of her heart would make her the greatest idiot in all of Britain.

She turned blindly into one of the side salons, and on spotting an unlit alcove, she quickly cloaked herself with its sheltering shadows. The darkness felt blessedly cool against her burning cheeks.

Another reminder of the folly of playing with fire.

Willing her heart to steady its erratic galloping, Harriet slowly regained a measure of control over her rebellious body. *Reason must rule.* It was imperative to assess the situation with her usual clear-headed clarity.

She took a moment to mentally review what she knew. After thinking more about the note she had found under Jack's chair, she had come to the conclusion that there were three stark facts to face—He must be in love with a lady named Camille... she was in some sort of trouble that had to do with the three names of the French émigré leaders here in London... Jack was searching for a way to help her.

Harriet was pragmatic enough to know she couldn't compete romantically with a sultry siren—Camille, being French, would naturally be beautiful and seductive. But as a salve to her wounded pride, she could at least prove to Jack that he was wrong to assume he didn't need her help. If she could find some important clue that would help solve his mystery, she might win his respect, if not his heart.

A small consolation, perhaps, but she liked the challenge of solving complicated conundrums, and it was far better than brooding like a lovesick mooncalf.

"Oh, here you are." Theo joined her in the shadows. "I was worried..." Her friend paused. "Good heavens, is something wrong?"

"I'm just fatigued," lied Harriet. "I'm not sure which was more exhausting—dodging Amirault's clumsy feet or enduring his ham-handed attempts to ingratiate himself with me because of my father's position in the government."

Theo clucked in sympathy. "I'm sorry you were forced to endure his company for so long. Did you see that Jack arrived not long ago? Perhaps a dance with him would help chase away your scowl. His company always seems to entertain you." An impish grin tugged at her lips. "The rest of us certainly enjoy your verbal duels."

Harriet chose to ignore the question. "I hope it wasn't too onerous for you to spend time with Beaumont."

"He was quite polite," replied Theo. "His compliments were typically Gallic—all outrageous flummeries and the like. But what lady doesn't like hearing such things, even if they aren't true."

What lady, indeed? thought Harriet. Careful to keep the note of wistfulness out of her voice, she responded, "A little flattery is always a balm for the spirits. Just as long as one doesn't take it to heart."

Theo let out a low laugh. "Oh, there is no chance of that. Like you, I am utterly pragmatic when it comes to romance. I'm not the sort of female men fall in love with. So I would never be so foolish as to dream of girlish dreams that can never be."

CHAPTER 7

"Jack."

He jerked his head up at the sound of Camille's soft whisper, relief warring with a burble of pent-up ire. He had left the ball early to arrive at the appointed rendezvous time and had been waiting for nearly an hour. "You're late—damnably late."

"I'm sorry, *cheri*." Camille took a seat and angled it deeper into the gloom of the tavern's ill-lit taproom. "But my time is not always my own."

Jack watched the nervous play of her slender fingers against the tabletop and then felt like a brute when his gaze caught the dark hollows below her eyes.

"Forgive me. I was on edge," he rasped. "Hell's teeth, I worry about you, alone and trying to deal with all this in enemy territory."

She looked away quickly, her hair falling to hide her face as she smoothed at a fold of her cloak.

He was a good enough soldier to recognize an evasive maneuver when he saw one.

"I am not alone, Jack. I've found an ally who has promised me that he has the influence to help me."

"Who?" he demanded softly, hoping his voice didn't betray his disappointment.

"I can't tell you that right now." A ragged exhale. "It is even more complicated than I first told you. There are factions within the Royalists."

"I am aware of that," he interrupted.

Camille twisted a lock of her hair around her finger, her eyes refusing to meet his. The fidgets made the silence between them even more strained.

Finally, she looked up. "Do you know a Miss Harriet Farnum?" she asked abruptly.

"What in the devil's name..." He paused, bewildered. "Yes, in fact I do, but why—"

"It's just that my friend had an idea," she answered quickly.

Friend? This ally was all of a sudden a friend? Jack felt something in his gut tighten. Not quite trusting his voice, he nodded for her to go on.

"He said that the two of you have a connection from child-hood and that her father is a diplomat working on sorting out what will happen to France if Napoleon is defeated. So he thought if I could meet him, and perhaps have a chance to explain my plight..."

"I thought you were adamant about not involving the British government."

"This would be personal, not official." A faint flush came to her cheeks. "I understand he is a widower..."

Jack fisted his hand but held himself back from banging it on the table. "Ye God," he muttered. "What would Pierre say to such madness?"

Camille lowered her lashes. "It is wartime, Jack. You know better than I that one must be pragmatic." Shadows flitted beneath the fringe of gold. "Sometimes principles must be sacrificed."

"But not honor," he shot back. "Never honor."

Her breath drew into her lungs with an audible rush. And then burst out as a ragged sob. "Now it is my turn to beg forgiveness." She pressed her palms to her eyes. "Of course you are right. I—I am not thinking straight." Her voice wavered. "I am so confused."

His insides unknotted. "Understandably so." Reaching out, he uncurled one of her hands and twined his fingers with hers. They were cold as ice.

"All the more reason to trust me to help," he said.

Camille shook her head in mute refusal.

Jack blew out a huff of frustration. "At least think it over, before doing anything rash," he asked. "You've stepped into a nest of vipers. Beware of their fangs."

She tried to rise, but he kept hold of her. "Just remember, snakes have very primitive brains. I've never known one to have any concept of friendship or loyalty."

"I must go, Jack."

This time, he released his grip. "When can we meet again?"

"I—I don't know." Camille drew the hood of her cloak up over her hair. "I'll send word to your townhouse."

Jack suspected it was a lie, but he was suddenly too tired to argue. "I am here whenever you need me."

A gust rattled the nearby window. As she melted into the darkness, he felt its chill seep through the glass and wrap around him.

Harriet was still uncertain as to whether she should have invited Theo to accompany her to Lady Catherine's weekly meeting. But on seeing her friend's excitement reflected back in the carriage windowpanes, she quickly swallowed any thought of expressing her reservations.

Patronizing apologies would be unwelcome. That had been made abundantly clear at Gunter's Tea Shop.

"I have been thinking about one of the essays I read." Theo turned away from the glass and for the next little while, as the carriage clattered eastward, proceeded to offer her impressions. "Will the group think me buffle-headed or naïve if I voice such things?" she asked hesitantly when she was done.

"Not at all," assured Harriet. "They will welcome your thoughts. The whole point of the discussion is to freely offer ideas. We all encourage each other to say what we feel without fear of criticism."

"How refreshing," mused Theo. "That is the exact opposite of the conversations that take place within the *ton*."

"So it is." The wheels slowed to a halt. "We're here."

After taking leave of her maid with the usual instructions, she led her friend across the square, quelling the lingering questions about her own judgment by reminding herself that in the past, Jack had taken delight in saying she was too practical and pragmatic to ever take any risks.

Ha! This was hardly the safe path to take, she thought as she guided Theo around a pile of pungent horse droppings.

Let us hope it doesn't lead to perdition.

Lady Catherine's warm welcome chased some of her worries away. The rest of the group greeted Theo with equal enthusiasm, and her friend's usual shyness with strangers couldn't help but give way to tentative smiles as she was drawn into the friendly bantering that always preceded the serious talk. The discussion, a continuation of what subjects girls ought to learn in school, proved quite lively, and Theo's comments sparked a number of interesting exchanges. By the time the sessions ended and tea was served, her friend's cheeks were pink with pleasure from all the compliments she had received.

"It is always a pleasure to meet a fellow female who knows how to use her brain for more than a perch for her bonnet, Lady Theo," murmured Miss Breville, the scholarly spinster. "I hope you will consider attending our meetings on a regular basis."

"Assuming our radical Bluestocking ideas haven't frightened you off," added Miss Ashmun with a grin.

"N-not at all," exclaimed Theo. "That is, I didn't mean—"

Mrs. Currough kindly cut off her stammering. "We know what you meant."

Theo shot her a grateful look. "I would very much like to come again, if you all don't mind."

The soft clinking of porcelain and silver punctuated pithy comments on the latest on-dits in the newspaper as they all enjoyed their refreshments. Then, when the platters of pastries had finished making their rounds, Miss Ashmun dusted her fingertips and leaned forward in her chair.

"I do hope you will consent to give us all another lesson in the art of beauty, Mrs. Currough."

The request was quickly seconded by the others.

"And I do hope Miss Farnam will be kind enough to serve as the, er..."

"Fool?" suggested Harriet.

Laughter greeted the quip.

"It does make some sense," observed the Irish Beauty. "Having someone serve as a model helps everyone to visualize what I am saying."

Harriet let out a sigh. "Very well." She paused, thinking of her friend's self-deprecating comments on her appearance. "But Lady Theo was extremely interested when I explained some of your advice, and if I am to make a cake of myself, I could use some moral support."

"Oh, no. I couldn't—" protested Theo.

"It's an excellent suggestion!" agreed Mrs. McNulty, signaling

Theo to rise. "It's good to have a variety of shapes and sizes to show what we mean."

"I doubt that even the great artistry of Madame Deauville can work any miracles on me," said Theo as she reluctantly stood up beside Harriet.

"Oh, you would be surprised at what a few bits of colored cloth can do, dearie." The renowned dressmaker slowly circled the two young ladies. "Hmmm."

Harriet gave an inward wince as the other woman tapped thoughtfully at her chin.

"Hmmm."

Theo's eyes widened as her walking gown was tugged and twitched.

"Stand up straighter, and pull your breadbox in and up," counseled Mrs. McNulty as she set her hand on her own midriff and exhaled. "Like so."

"Why, that's remarkable," murmured Miss Ashmun. "It makes a noticeable difference."

"As we said last week, the art of beauty is all about creating illusion," said Mrs. Currough. She, too, circled Harriet and Theo, stopping to make a few adjustments in the angle of a chin or a shoulder. "But aside from using physical sleights of hand, you must also use your mind to your advantage."

Theo made a wry face. "No matter how hard I think, it's not as if I am going to transform myself into a Diamond of the First Water."

"On the contrary," said the Irish beauty. "That is exactly what you can do."

"How?" blurted out Theo.

"It's really quite simple. By believing you are the most beautiful, desirable woman in the world."

Everyone in the room regarded Mrs. Currough with openmouthed surprise.

"Aye, it's true," confirmed Mrs. McNulty. "With a little help from the likes of me, of course."

"I can't," whispered Theo. "It's... absurd."

"I have to agree," said Harriet. By any stretch of the imagination, bricks were neither beautiful nor desirable. "I know you said beauty comes from within, and it did seem last week that an air of self-confidence did add a certain spring to my step. But a Diamond of the First Water?" She shook her head. "Surely that's impossible."

Mrs. Currough didn't answer right away. Turning her back to the room, she moved closer to the window and appeared to be studying some distant point across the square.

Harriet and Theo exchanged guilty looks. Someone coughed.

The small sound seemed to rouse the Irish beauty. She spun around and as the sunlight fell on her face, a collective gasp rose from the group.

As if by magic, she appeared utterly transformed.

Harriet stared in wonder. It was impossible to describe the change in words. Her eyes, her smile, her body looked the same—and yet completely altered.

"How did you do that?" she demanded. "Some black magic potion in the tea?"

"Nothing nearly so dramatic," answered Mrs. Currough. "When I see myself as an Incomparable, so do you."

"It can't be as easy as that," protested Theo.

"There are details that can be added to heighten the aura of allure, like silks, and scents. But the essence comes from within."

Harriet thought back on the earlier lesson. "It's one thing to *act* like a princess. I admit, those subtle little changes in posture and movement made a difference." *Why, even Jack had noticed.* "However, it's quite beyond the realm of possibility to *believe* I am a princess."

An enigmatic smile played on the Irish beauty's lips. "Why?"

"Because it is not true," she answered.

"Ah, truth." A sparkle of mischief seemed to light in the other woman's eyes. "In my experience, that is no easy thing to define." A saucy wink. "Indeed, I think it far more elusive than the morals of a mistress."

Titters of nervous laughter floated through the room.

"Truth," continued Mrs. Currough, "is far from absolute. Like so many things in life, it depends on your perspective and preconceptions."

Having witnessed the workings of the diplomatic world from childhood on, Harriet conceded the elemental wisdom of the observation.

"So what you are saying," ventured Theo, "is we should create our own definitions of beauty and allure."

"Precisely," replied Mrs. Currough.

Theo gave a wry grimace. "I'll likely appear a complete nodcock, but I'll try." Squeezing her eyes shut, she drew in several deep breaths, then let her lids flutter open and smiled.

Good Heavens. Harriet blinked. Perhaps the power of self-persuasion was more potent than she had imagined.

"Excellent," murmured Mrs. McNulty. "Now take a turn around the tea table, imagining that some special alchemy in the chandelier is pulling the crown of your head up to the ceiling."

"Very interesting." Miss Breville jotted down a few lines in her notebook.

Mrs. Currough fixed Harriet with an inquiring look, and beneath the glint of humor it held a spark of challenge.

Casting off her misgivings, she decided it was only fair that she try to match Theo's efforts.

For the next quarter hour, she and her friend did their best to put Mrs. Currough's advice into practice, and though hoots of laughter rose on occasion, the session ended with a round of spontaneous applause from the rest of the group.

"That was most enlightening," said Miss Ashmun with a dreamy sigh. She, too, had been taking notes.

Their two instructors made one last circle around them before retreating to a spot by the bow-front window. The discussion, pitched too low for anyone else to overhear, went on for an alarmingly long time.

"I fear I may be too great a test of their skills," whispered Theo.

"Nonsense," replied Harriet stoutly. "You already appear transformed."

"I—I do?" She craned her neck, trying to catch a glimpse of her reflection in the glass windowpanes.

"Stop fidgeting," ordered Harriet. "Remember what they told us—a beauty never betrays a soupcon of doubt."

"Right, right."

It was Mrs. McNulty who broke off the talk to approach them. "The two of you have an appointment at Madame Deauville's shop tomorrow afternoon at precisely 3."

"We've an appointment?" repeated Theo faintly. "W-With you, the most exclusive modiste in all of London?"

"Yes. And please do not be late. I've a very crowded schedule for the next few weeks, given Lady Henning's upcoming gala ball."

"I fear such a meeting may be casting pearls before swine," murmured Harriet. "I have no idea how to choose styles, colors, fabrics or trimmings."

"Which is why you will leave all of that to us," said Mrs. Currough, moving with an impossibly elegant *swish-swish* of her silken skirts.

"But—"

The Irish beauty raised a slender finger, and Harriet fell silent. "Your skills at arguing need no polishing, Miss Farnum. But in this matter you must trust us."

"Implicitly," added Mrs. McNulty, her gaze turning a bit steely. "Without so much as a peep of protest."

Harriet hesitated. Ceding control of such an intimately

personal matter was not an easy matter. But after casting a downward glance at the profusion of lilac ribbons her maid had decided to add to her bodice, she gave a grim nod.

GROWLING AN INPATIENT OATH, Jack rapped the big brass knocker again. *Maps, regimental lists, area commandants*—he had a sheaf of documents stuffed in his pocket. The information passed over by his friend at Horse Guards was proving devilishly hard to sort out on his own, but it had suddenly occurred to him who had just the organizational skills to lend a hand.

"Milord?" A tall, reedy butler opened the door and peered down his long nose.

"Halloo, Bailin. Please send word up to Harry that I need to speak with her."

"If you will follow me to the West Parlor, sir, I shall inquire as to whether Miss Farnum is at home."

"Oh, come, let us not stand on ceremony. I saw John Coachman in the mews and he told me she returned a half hour ago."

Bailin gave a long-suffering sniff. "I see I shall have to have a word with him about gossiping about the family."

"Don't fly up in the boughs. I'm almost family." He grinned. "Tell her to hurry—oh, and have Cook send out a platter of her famous gingersnaps."

The butler inclined a formal bow, but not before Jack caught a twitch of his thin-set lips.

"What has you in such pucker?" demanded Harriet a few minutes later as she hurried into the parlor. "Bailin seemed to think you have something important on your mind." She glanced at the platter of pastries. "Or were you simply starving for sweets?"

Jack finished the last bite of his biscuit. "I miss Cook's confections."

"Your cousin makes wonderful chocolate creations," she pointed out. "Surely he left your father's cook some of the recipes."

"Yes, but Rafe's recipes are inspired by love." He exaggerated a grimace. "So they are not quite to my taste."

Harriet laughed, but an odd undertone seemed to roughen the sound. "Nor mine." She took a seat on the sofa. "But I imagine you haven't come here to discuss culinary matters."

"Correct." He slouched down beside her and drew the low tea table closer. Their knees touched as he shifted position. She flinched, as if some frisson of fire had scorched through her skirts. Strangely enough, he had felt it, too. The tension coiled inside him must be setting off unexpected sparks.

"Sorry," he muttered, shifting again to pull the papers from his pockets. His long legs suddenly felt awkward and impossible to arrange. Setting the documents on the table, he took a moment to smooth out the folds. "I thought you might enjoy helping me piece together a puzzle."

"A puzzle," she repeated. "Why would you think that?"

Jack cleared his throat. "Well, er..." *Because you are clever, smart and imaginative.* "Because you always ran circles around me and William when it came to figuring out how patterns fit together."

When she didn't reply with her usual barbed humor, he went on, "Dash it all, Harry, are you still brooding over the brick comment?"

That roused her from silence. "Of course I'm not brooding over bricks. As you pointed out, I'm far too solid and sensible for that."

Damnation. This new prickliness was a puzzle even more diabolically difficult to sort out than the documents.

"Forgive my feeble brain for failing to comprehend the problem," he said slowly. "But I have always been under the impression that you liked being thought of as solid and sensible. What has changed?"

"Nothing," snapped Harriet. She plucked at a loose thread on her bodice, then smoothed at the rumpled folds of her skirts.

The ripple of color suddenly distracted him from the subject at hand. That particular shade of russet, he observed, did nothing to compliment the glorious copper highlights in her chestnut hair.

"If I am so solid and sensible, why is it you've shoved me aside from whatever mystery it is you are investigating?" she asked abruptly.

"I told you," Jack muttered. "I don't want to take any chances of you getting hurt."

"First of all, the Royalists may fight among themselves, but I highly doubt they would dare resort to violence against any members of the *ton*," replied Harriet. "Secondly, I am sensible enough to be able to take care of myself. And thirdly, if there truly is danger, then you ought to have someone watching your back."

"There is a great difference between being sensible and being experienced," he countered. "I'm a soldier. I'm trained to deal with danger."

Harriet stared pointedly at his chest. It felt as if her steely gaze were cutting through the layers of fabric and knifing across his scarred flesh. "No amount of training or experience can parry those moments of chance or fate that happen in the heat of battle. You know that better than anyone."

Most of his acquaintances he could deflect with either humor or cynicism. Not Harriet. Damn her for being the one person brutally honest enough and unflinching enough to make him face his own vulnerabilities.

The papers crackled as his hand swept over the dog-eared corners and pushed them back into a pile. "Never mind. I will find someone else to help." Jack drew in a ragged breath, surprised at how disappointed he felt at the idea. "Someone who won't natter at me."

She seized his wrist, her curling fingers soft and warm where they slipped from his starched cuff to touch his skin. "I *never* natter. I may rail or harangue, but not natter."

Against his will, he found himself smiling. "You forgot badger."

"I left it out on purpose. Badgers aren't terribly attractive creatures. It's bad enough being a brick."

A hint of laughter rippled through the depths of her sea-dark eyes, and all at once its current seemed to hold his gaze in thrall. How was it that he had never noticed the infinite range of blues swirling beneath her lashes—azure, cerulean and subtle shades that defied a name.

He meant to pull away, but somehow not a muscle twitched.

It was Harriet who hitched back and let her hand fall away. "So, we have a puzzle. Three Royalists under suspicion, a mystery you won't explain to me, and these..." She pointed to the papers. "Which contain Heaven knows what." Her lips pursed. "If you expect me to see any patterns, you are giving me precious little to go on."

"Actually, it's only the papers that hold the puzzle. There's something hidden within the interminable list of dates, transfers, military units and the like."

"What?" she asked.

"A missing soldier."

"Can you be more specific?"

Jack flicked a few crumbs from his sleeve. "A French officer. His friends have been told he's being held somewhere in England on parole. But so far, they have uncovered no record of his existence. I hope the answer lies in these military records. It will be tedious work, cross-checking references and transfer orders, looking at the maps which record the different parole areas, and that sort of thing. I haven't the eye or the patience to make sense of it."

"I see," murmured Harriet, as she began flipping through the pages.

"There is more," he said after a moment. She had very lovely hands, graceful and capable, as opposed to the flighty movements of so many other young ladies of the *ton.*

"I expected as much." Harriet looked up. "It will take some time to organize it all. How soon can you get the other material to me?"

"Within the hour."

"I am assuming you would like to learn your missing officer's whereabouts as soon as possible."

He nodded.

"I have a previous engagement for tomorrow—and I cannot alter it. But I'll try to have it by the day after,"

"Harry, you are—"

"Don't you *dare* say it," she murmured.

"You are," he continued, "an Incomparable—a singular lady of unique talents."

A quicksilver spasm of emotion passed over her features, too fleeting to discern. Shock, no doubt, at hearing him capable of composing gentlemanly words.

He grinned. "You see, I can manage a proper compliment if I try very hard."

"Don't exhaust yourself," replied Harriet dryly. And yet a peculiar sort of light lingered in her gaze. "Clearly you have far more serious matters weighing on your mind."

CHAPTER 8

"*O*xfordshire," muttered Harriet after consulting several documents and then looking back at the map of military districts. "Jack's French friend *has* to be in Oxfordshire."

She had been up since dawn studying the sheaf of official papers. Names of the prisoners were not listed, but by methodically tracing the movements of captured officers through the various checkpoints, she had figured out which group had come from the battle Jack had mentioned and where they had been sent to serve their parole.

Pushing back her chair, Harriet steepled her fingers and mulled over the matter. She would, of course, go over her notes to be absolutely sure she hadn't missed anything. However, she was confident the man's whereabouts was now pinned down.

Far less clear was Jack's pressing concern. A friend, he had said. And yet, the note she had found under his chair seemed to indicate he was involved in this mystery because of a lady named Camille.

"I *am* good at piecing together puzzles," she said, tapping her fingertips together. "But in this I am having a deucedly difficult time trying to discern any pattern."

Tap, tap, tap. Several more minutes of contemplation brought no brilliant flash of illumination. Expelling a sigh, she glanced at the mantel clock, and then shifted the different piles into an orderly row on her desk. Jack's conundrum would have to wait.

Because Madame Deauville would not.

~

"Oooh, THIS IS AWFULLY EXCITING." Theo peeked through the windowpane as the carriage clattered to a halt in front of an elegant shop at the top of Bond Street. "I feel as if I have a flock of butterflies flitting around inside my stomach."

Harriet said nothing, but she, too, was experiencing a sense of nervous anticipation. It was foolish to be in a pucker over a few yards of fabric. She had always thought of fashion as frivolous...

"Mama will fall into a fit of megrims if I end up attired in anything other than lemon or peach pastels," intoned Theo.

"No she won't," assured Harriet. "Your mother wouldn't dare question Madame Deauville's sense of style. She wants you to attract a husband, preferably a wealthy, titled one, so she'll be in alt that the most exclusive modiste in London has consented to design a wardrobe for you."

Theo sat back. "Why do you think Mrs. McNulty offered to help? I've heard that these fancy dressmakers are very discerning about which clients to accept. Their reputations depend on ladies looking marvelous in their creations—and I'm hardly the sort who will show clothes to any advantage."

"Because she is nice," answered Harriet firmly. "And because we are going to appear far more beautiful and alluring than any of the Diamonds of the First Water, remember?"

Theo forced a weak smile. "Right, right."

Despite her own trepidations, she walked briskly to the shop's ornate door and pushed it open.

At the tinkling of the bell, one of Madame's assistants looked up from straightening the stacks of pattern books. As she eyed the pair's unfashionable garments, her smile turned to a smirk. "*Alors*, I am very sorry, but Madame Deauville doesn't accept any clients without a recommendation and an interview." An audible sniff. "And most certainly not without an appointment—"

"*Bonjour*, Miss Farnum! Bonjour, Lady Theo!" The very picture of Parisian savvy and sophistication, Mrs. McNulty emerged from behind a burgundy-colored velvet curtain, wearing her persona of Madame Deauville like a perfectly tailored ballgown. Not a loose stitch or thread marred the perfection of her performance.

"Marie-Claire, please prepare the West fitting room for my friends."

The girl continued to stare, her nose crinkling as if someone had flung a piece of bad fish into the shop.

"*Tout de suite!*" An impatient clap-clap finally sent her scurrying.

"Lazy slug," muttered Mrs. McNulty under her breath. "But I keep her because she's the only one of the lot of us who speaks perfect French. The other girls all learn their accents from her."

Harriet glanced around the main showroom, taking in the elegant appointments, the gilt-framed mirrors, the Louis XIV furniture, and the exquisite gowns discreetly displayed on mannequins between the folded samples of rich fabrics. Her gaze then fell on the insipid shade of her own dowdy walking dress, a color that was somewhere between biscuit and taupe.

No wonder poor Marie-Claire had looked a little queasy.

Next to her, Theo sucked in her breath. "Oh," was all she managed to say.

"Come, come, I'll give you a tour later, but I have my senior patternmaker waiting for you." Mrs. McNulty consulted the gold watch pinned to her bosom. "And we have limited time in which to work with her."

She quickly shepherded Harriet and Theo into a spacious

room, where a quartet of girls holding an array of pin cushions, scissors and long strips of pale muslin stood waiting to one side of the raised square platform that was set in the middle of the space. On the other side was a diminutive older woman sporting the largest pair of pinch-nez Harriet had ever seen. The over-sized lenses and small, beaky nose gave the stranger the expression of a startled owl.

"I was just mentioning to Mademoiselle Franchot what styles I envision for you two," said Mrs. McNulty. "But now she can decide for herself whether I am right."

"Mmmph."

Harriet thought that was a rather unpromising sound.

"*Oui, oui,*" added Mademoiselle Franchot in a gruff voice. "I can't argue with your discerning eye." She unwound the tape measure wrapped around her bony wrist. "I would just suggest a few minor alterations to take into account—"

A squeak of alarm interrupted the exchange as a young seamstress pushed through the draperies, arms flapping in agitation. "Celine asks that you come quickly, Madame. The duchess is upset over the fit of her bodice."

"Then perhaps she ought not to consume half a dozen cream cakes for breakfast each day," muttered Mrs. McNulty. "Please excuse us for a moment," she said to Harriet and Theo.

"But of course," they chorused.

"Molly, you had better come too." Her gaze took on the flash of sharpened steel. "I trust this won't take long, ladies."

"I would not care to cause a fuss within her shop," whispered Theo after the two women had marched out of the room.

"I doubt that even a duchess will dare to throw a fit of vapors," answered Harriet. "Not with Lady Henning's gala taking place next week."

The quartet of assistants had dutifully trooped after Mrs. McNulty and the head seamstress, leaving the two of them alone in the fitting room. Curiosity impelled Harriet to move out into the curtained corridor, closer to the heavy velvet, and twitch back a tiny opening, allowing a peek into the main display salon. She had never given much thought to fashion, but the array of gorgeous fabrics, styles and trimmings were tantalizing.

Attired in such finery, would she really feel like a princess with the power to captivate men with her radiant beauty? She felt a flutter in her chest, then quickly reminded herself that enchantments were the stuff of fairie tales. And she, of all people, was far too practical and pragmatic to confuse make-believe with real life.

"It's all so beautiful," intoned Theo, who had crept up to join her. They both stood very still, simply taking in all the lush details of the shimmering silks, the gossamer laces and profusion of delicately-colored ribbons.

Harriet found her eye drawn to the display table where a shop assistant was carefully refolding a stack of feather light Kashmir shawls. The swirling paisley patterns of deep jeweltone colors made her long to wrap one around her bare shoulders and see if it were truly as soft as a baby's breath.

A sigh slipped from her lips, only to be lost in the muted ring of the entrance bell. As the assistant turned to greet the new customers, Harriet heard Theo make a strangled sound.

Shifting her gaze, she immediately saw why. Mrs. Currough had entered the shop—accompanied by Jack and James.

"Perhaps we should withdraw," said Theo, her cheeks slowly turning a mottled red. "It would be awfully mortifying if they should spot us."

"*We* have nothing to be ashamed of," replied Harriet, even though she knew her friend was right about the embarrassment of being caught peeping. Still, like a moth drawn to a flame, she found she couldn't break away.

James and Jack appeared to be having an animated exchange with the Irish Beauty. Harriet couldn't make out their words, but the laughs and smiles spoke eloquently. She felt a gritty dryness form in the back of her throat as the trio pulled down pattern books and began to peruse the various styles. Suddenly the display room lost all its magic. Her spirits came plummeting back to earth.

"But on second thought, you're right," she whispered to her friend, hoping to hide the pinch in her voice. "It would not be dignified to be caught spying like naughty schoolgirls." Drawing the velvet back into place, she retreated back to the fitting area, wishing that she might flee much farther... preferably to Bombay or Xanadu, whichever was the greatest distance from London and a dark-haired gentleman with the devil's own smile.

Thankfully, Theo seemed to have sunk into a subdued mood as well. They each took a seat on the two hard-back chairs not piled high with paper patterns and pin boxes and waited in silence for Mrs. McNulty to return.

But to Harriet's dismay, it was Mrs. Currough who pushed through the burgundy draperies several minutes later.

"Betty invited me to come offer my advice on colors and decorative detail." She said breezily as she unfastened her elegant pelisse and hung it from one of the brass clothes pegs. "I trust you won't feel that too many cooks will spoil the broth."

Harriet mumbled a curt reply.

"I have some ideas as to what hues will look best," went on the Irish Beauty. "But of course it's always wise to see how they look in different light." Off came her kidskin gloves. "This will be great fun."

Harriet nodded, unable to bring herself to look up from the floor.

Theo was equally quiet.

Mrs. Currough's brows arched in mild surprise. She busied herself for a moment in straightening out the patterns and fabric samples, then inquired, "Are you two nervous?"

"No," answered Harriet quickly.

"Ah." More bustling. "Then might I inquire what has you so Friday-faced?"

"N-nothing." She tried to force a smile, but found her face felt stiff as stone. "Nothing at all."

At that, the Irish Beauty turned and set a hand on her hip. "I would not last very long in my profession if I were unable to read the subtle mood shifts of those around me." Her lips quirked. "And yours, my dear, is hardly subtle."

"It's nothing important." Aware of how false her voice sounded, Harriet added, "That is, it's nothing that I care to talk about."

Mrs. Currough's gaze turned even more pensive. Harriet had the uncomfortable sensation that it could penetrate to the shadowed places deep within—places that even she didn't dare to explore.

"I see." The Irish Beauty slanted a look at Theo and then at the draperies. "Would this 'nothing' perchance have to do with my interlude with Lord Osborne and Lord Leete?"

Harriet's throat felt too tight to answer.

The silence was apparently far more eloquent than words.

Perching a hip on the tea table, Mrs. Currough folded her hands in her lap. "I happened to encounter the gentlemen as I was coming from my carriage. We have met at several parties and are acquaintances."

Close acquaintances, no doubt, thought Harriet. The knot in his stomach tightened, and tears prickled against the insides of her eyelids as suddenly the idea that she might ever be alluring seemed absurd. How could she ever hope to compete with an Irish Beauty or a sultry French siren?

"Lord Osborne and Lord Leete are perfectly free to form any friendships they so choose," she said stiffly. "It can be of no concern to me."

"And yet it is," said Mrs. Currough gently.

Harriet felt her defenses crumble in the face of such kindness.

"O-Only because it makes me realize how foolish it is to think a plain, outspoken hellion like me could ever master the art of appearing alluring." She swallowed hard. "Not that I wish to appear alluring to them. I've known them both since childhood and they think of me as naught but the pesky little sister of their schoolfriend."

Understanding seemed to glimmer in the other woman's eyes. "I have a feeling they will soon learn to look at both of you in a new light."

Theo straightened her slumped shoulders. "But I... I..."

Mrs. Currough cut off her stammering. "Just to clear up any misconceptions, your gentlemen friends asked my advice on a gift—for Lord Osborne's sister. She has a birthday coming and he wanted to give her a special gown."

"Oh," croaked Harriet and Theo in unison.

"But as neither of them knows satin from sarcenet, they appealed to me to help them pick out a style."

"You must think me a complete nodcock for acting like such an idiot," stammered Harriet.

"Be assured that we all act like idiots over men." A wry smile blossomed on the Irish Beauty's lips. "Though I'm not sure they deserve it."

Her pithy humor seemed to dispel the dark cloud hanging over the room. Harriet laughed and was quickly joined by Theo.

"But we females have a way of getting our revenge." She rose with a sensuous whispering of lace and silk. "We can drive them to distraction with our airs of mystery and grace." She tapped a fingertip to her forehead. "But as I've told you before, the belief must come from within. The rest is easy."

"But what if I don't feel mysterious," asked Theo.

"Like all skills, it takes practice," replied the Irish Beauty. Mrs. McNulty's voice punctuated the sound of approaching steps in the corridor. "And now is a good time to begin."

"The duchess has finally been put in her place," announced the dressmaker as she stomped into the room. "Though I was sorely tempted to consign her to the hottest hole in Hades." Taking up a handful of shimmering silks, she held them up to the light. "Now, let us turn our hands to more pleasant tasks. Mrs. Currough, what do you think of this smoky emerald color for Miss Farnum..."

JACK TOOK a grateful gulp of sherry. He and James had been ushered into the private parlor reserved for gentlemen patrons, and a shop assistant had served refreshments. "Ye Gods, who would have guessed that fashion is so bloody complicated," he groused. "Is there really such a thing as a mutton sleeve, or was the seamstress just pulling my leg?"

"I have no idea." James downed his drink in one swallow. "Georgie had better appreciate the sacrifices I make for her." Staring into the empty glass, he grimaced. "Wellington could probably outfit a regiment of Hussars with what I paid for one ballgown."

"Apparently Madame Deauville is the most exclusive dressmaker in Town, so I imagine she can charge a king's ransom. I'm told ladies are willing to do most anything short of murder to win a place on her very limited list of clients."

"Knowing how seriously ladies are about appearing stylish, I'm not sure murder isn't in the realm of possibility," quipped James.

Jack went to the sideboard to refill their glasses. His friend's harried chuckle seemed to stir an echo. It came again—a light, melodious sound that tugged his mouth up at the corners. Cocking an ear, he paused to listen.

Yes, definitely laughter. Something about its ring tickled against his consciousness, and he found himself thinking of Harriet. Which was a contradiction if ever there was one. Harriet didn't give a fig for fancy dresses. She was, he conceded, anything but stylish. Neither the colors nor the cut of her clothes did her any favors, but somehow what he pictured now in his mind's eye was the curl of her smile and the sparkle of mischief in her eyes...

"Halloooo!"

Jack's head snapped around. "Er, what?"

"I said, stop woolgathering and bring me my drink. Shopping works up a great thirst."

"Sorry." Jack lingered for a moment longer, listening to the muffled notes fade away. After pouring a generous splash of spirits, he shook off his reveries and rejoined his friend. "Do you care what a lady is wearing?" he asked abruptly.

"No," James flashed an evil grin. "I'm far more interested in what she's *not* wearing."

"Finish your sherry," said Jack. "Then I suggest we quit this henhouse and head to White's, where they serve something more potent than these dainty feminine tipples." He suddenly felt in need of something fiery to drown the disquieting sense of unease that had started to churn in his belly.

It was worry over Camille, he told himself. But loath though he was to admit it, thoughts of her had been tangled of late, his loyalties stretched and a little frayed by her evasiveness. If only Harriet could pin down some answers, perhaps that would help dispel the uncertainties.

James thumped down his empty glass. "An excellent suggestion. Let us go." He rose from the leather armchair. "Before they think of a way to squeeze another guinea out of me."

They headed down the corridor leading to the side entrance, the heavy draperies of the fitting rooms stirring in soft undulations as they passed.

"What arcane feminine transformations take place behind those bits of velvet remain a complete mystery to me," murmured James.

"There is much about the female mind that is baffling," replied

Jack, thinking of Camille. "Perhaps it's best that we don't know all the frightening details."

Lapsing into a pensive silence, he and his friend quickened their steps. They had just turned the corner when up ahead, the fabric fluttered wildly and two ladies emerged from one of the inner sanctums amid a flurry of cheery waves and goodbyes.

"Oh!" Harriet's smile gave way to wide-eyed surprise.

Harriet?

Jack blinked, wondering if his eyes were deceiving him. "What are *you* doing here?" he blurted out.

"Shopping," she replied.

"But you never..."

Her chin rose a notch.

"Er, that is..."

"That is lovely," finished James smoothly. "Did you find something that pleased you?"

"Yes," responded Harriet in a tone that seemed to dare him to challenge her. "I purchased a new shawl."

Jack decided to stay silent.

"And you, Lady Theo?" asked James politely.

"I did as well," she said softly.

The four of them stood for a moment in awkward shuffling until Harriet abruptly took his arm. "Might you escort us out to our carriage? I was going to send a note to your townhouse, but since you are here, I have some further information about... the matter we've been discussing."

James promptly placed Theo's gloved hand on his sleeve and turned their steps for the door.

Jack waited until they had stepped outside before moving to follow them. "Well?" he asked eagerly.

"I am almost certain your missing officer is in Oxfordshire. I need to do a bit more research and rechecking the lists to be sure, but my instincts tell me I'm right."

"Your instincts are usually bang on the mark," he mused. "My thanks, Harry."

She kept her gaze looking straight ahead. "Give me another day or two to confirm it. There is, of course, no guarantee that I've found your man. The transfers use numbers, not names. But going on the information you've given me it's the best I can do."

"It's hugely helpful," Jack assured her, slanting a sidelong glance to try to read her profile. It wasn't often that Harriet's voice gave nothing away.

"I am always happy when I prove helpful." *Was there an undertone of something sharper than her usual irony?* Of late, her moods had become strangely quixotic.

He was still watching her face as they passed from the subdued light of the corridor into the brilliance of the cloudless day. "You..." he began, only to find his attention captivated by the shawl draped around her shoulders. The subtle play of patterns and colors had come to life in the dancing, diamond-bright sunshine.

"You are looking very well in your new purchase," he murmured slowly, as his eyes adjusted to the glittering light. "Those colors suit you—they bring out the sparks in your hair."

"Sparks?" Harriet raised her brows.

"Yes, flame red ones, as well as burnt orange, dark bronze, and, well, all sorts of shades I can't name."

"Good heavens, you make me sound like Athena, the Goddess of War," she quipped.

"Yes, Athena—that suits you as well." He smiled. "Seeing as the ancient Greeks also considered her the Goddess of Wisdom."

It might only have been the reflection of the sun off the finely-woven wool, but it seemed like a blush had crept up to her cheeks.

"Have you ever wondered," she asked slowly, "why the Greeks made their Gods and Goddesses so complicated?"

It was likely meant as a distraction, not a question, and yet he found himself answering. "Mayhap because they recognized that all of us mere mortals have the same sort of conflicting natures tangled in our heads."

Harriet turned to face him, surprise quickly segueing into an inscrutable expression. She looked about to reply, but seemed to reconsider. Instead, she merely said, "I'll send you final word as soon I'm confident that the lists have yielded all their secrets to me."

CHAPTER 9

The parlor maid cleared her throat with a discreet cough. "Excuse me, Miss."

Harriet reluctantly looked up from the piles of papers on her desk.

"This arrived for you in the afternoon post."

Repressing an oath, she accepted the letter. Interruptions were always unwelcome when she was in the middle of sorting out a conundrum. However, a glance at the handwriting quelled her irritation. Lady Catherine never sent a missive simply to engage in idle chatter. There would be a good reason for it.

"Thank you, Mary." She quickly cracked the wax seal and read over the page. After thinking for a moment, Harriet set it aside and rose from her chair. "Kindly ask Ellie to bring down my cloak and have the carriage summoned. I need to go out on an errand."

Lady Catherine was writing an essay for one of the reform-minded newspapers and needed several books on political philosophy from her father's library in order to finish it. A servant could have delivered them, but Harriet preferred that her association with Red Lion Square didn't become common knowledge among the household staff. Her father, while an extremely tolerant parent, was a respected member of the government, and her involvement with a radical-thinking women's group—especially one that included a notorious courtesan and members of the working class—was something she would rather he didn't know. As for her maid and John Coachman, they were loyal friends—and enjoyed their ices at Gunter's too much to think of grassing on her.

Hurrying to the library, Harriet quickly located the books. Ellie, with her usual efficiency, was waiting by the front door.

"Might I inquire where you are off to, Miss Farnum?" asked the butler.

"Just a few errands, Bailin," replied Harriet breezily. "I shall be back in a trice."

"If your father returns—"

"My father mentioned this morning at breakfast that he is likely to be at the ministry until after midnight," she assured him. "There is no need for Cook to prepare supper. I'll simply have a cold collation."

A slight frown pinched between his brows, but he merely nodded.

The carriage ride passed quickly, as her coachman avoided the main thoroughfares in favor of the more lightly-traveled side streets. Harriet had already told him she would walk to her friend's townhouse through a series of quiet lanes just north of the square, which allowed the vehicle to wait where it was well-hidden from prying eyes.

"I shan't be long," she told Ellie.

"Ye sure I shouldn't come with you?"

"As I've told you before, I'm less conspicuous traveling without a maid. My cloak hides my face, and though it's a little rougher than Mayfair, it's not a dangerous area."

It was only a short sojourn through the deserted lanes and she cut quickly through a passageway leading out to the unpruned garden facing Lady Catherine's residence. Her friend was delighted to receive the books and tried to press her to stay for tea and cakes. But Harriet, anxious to finish her work for Jack, demurred.

"I really must go," she explained. "Like you, I have some important things to finish."

"Very well," answered Lady Catherine, though she did insist on giving her a half dozen copies of *La Belle Assemble*, London's most popular fashion magazine, to peruse at home. "But I shall insist that you and Theo give a full report of your fittings at Madame Deauville's establishment when next we meet."

"It was... very educational," answered Harriet. "I have no doubt that the gowns will be beautiful, but as to whether I can carry them off—"

"Nonsense, my dear. You will do marvelously well. I am sure of it."

Harriet wished she felt as confident, but kept any further doubts to herself. Excusing herself once again, she hurried down to the street and retraced her steps along the perimeter of the square.

The afternoon shadows had lengthened, the jagged shapes cast by the buildings making the passageway seem narrower, and a little forbidding. Jack's recent hints of danger swirling around his mystery must have her imagination on edge. Determined to quash such silly misgivings, she entered at a brisk pace. It was, she reminded herself, only a matter of minutes before she would reach the waiting carriage.

Rounding the first of several twisting turns, Harriet was aware of an unnatural stillness. It was quiet—too quiet. In contrast, the thump of her shoes on the rough cobbles seemed to echo like cannon fire off the surrounding brick and stone.

"The devil take it, stop acting like a flighty peagoose," she muttered, seeking to steady her jumpy nerves. "I've been in far worse hellholes than this in my travels."

Thump, thump. As if to mock her efforts, the echoes grew louder.

Harriet slowed as she approached the next bend, the tiny hairs on the back of her neck now standing on end.

Suddenly an oath rang out, followed by a thrashing flurry of punches, and then a sharp grunt of pain.

Acting on pure, primal instinct, she bolted forward and skidded through the turn.

Just up ahead, a man lay slumped on the ground. One of his attackers was on his knees, trying to staunch the blood streaming from his broken nose. The other was raising his arm.

A wink of steel pierced the gloom.

"Stop, you curs!" she cried.

The footpad with the knife spat out an oath. But his momentary hesitation gave Harriet just time enough to gather her wits. Aware of the weight of the fashion publications in her reticule, she swung it overhead and let it fly.

The missile caught him flush on the forehead, knocking him arse over teakettle into a puddle of muck. The weapon clattered away into the shadows.

Spooked, Broken Nose scrabbled to his feet. Grabbing his dazed cohort, he pulled him to his feet and the two of them fled down one of the side alleys.

Hitching in a breath, Harriet all at once felt a little lightheaded as the realization of what a mad, mad risk she had taken flooded over her. But another groan from the fallen man warned that she didn't have time for a fit of vapors.

He was hurt—the question was, how badly?

"Sir?" Kneeling down, she tentatively touched his coat. Her fingers came away smudged with blood.

An incoherent mutter. He was trying to speak.

"Lie still," cautioned Harriet, placing her palm on his chest. "I need to assess the damage."

Ignoring her sensible suggestion, the man squirmed under her touch and managed to lift his head. "Damnation, Harry! If you *ever* do anything half so foolish again, I swear, I'll take a birch to your backside."

Her hands fisted in the folds of his shirt as a spasm of pain passed over Jack's lips, pinching off further words. "We'll argue over who is the greater fool later," she replied calmly, although her insides were twisting into a knot of fear. "But for now, let me see how deeply that miscreant's blade cut into you."

"It's naught but a scratch," growled Jack. "I'm rather an expert when it comes to judging wounds from sharpened steel."

She started to unbutton his shirt and was flustered to find her hands were shaking. "That's *not* amusing."

A grunt. "It wasn't meant to be."

"Stop squirming." Slipping her fingers beneath the finespun linen, Harriet gently traced the line of his collarbone.

He went very still.

"That's better." His skin was warm and as she drew her touch lower, the coarse curls of hair peppering his chest tickled against her flesh. *So this is what a man feels like.* The sensation was infinitely intriguing. Flattening her palm to fit his shape, she drew slow, circling strokes over the solid contours of muscle.

"Lower," Jack said through gritted teeth.

"W-What?"

"Feel a little lower. The blade nicked over a rib," he replied. "If you'll just take the handkerchief out of my coat pocket, fold it over the wound, and then give me a hand up, instead of fussing like a mother hen, I'll be on my way."

Harriet forced his shoulders down. "Don't be a gudgeon. You'll end up flat on your face after several steps." Her gaze moved from his ashen cheeks to the spreading crimson stain on the snowy linen. "You've lost a lot of blood. I need to summon a doctor."

"*No!*" he exclaimed, the force of the protest sending another spasm twisting over his features. "No fuss. Need to keep this quiet." He looked up at her, shadows scudding beneath the fringe of his dark lashes. "Please."

"Very well." She thought for a moment. "Let me staunch the bleeding. Then, if you can manage to stay upright by leaning on me, I think I can get you to my friend's townhouse. It's not far."

"But—"

"The wound needs to be cleaned and bandaged, Jack."

"I tell you, I won't have a physician."

"You," muttered Harriet, "are an ass." Huffing a sigh, she added, "I'm perfectly capable of tending to it. I've patched up Wills more times than I can count, not to speak of having dealt with plenty of injuries on Papa's diplomatic missions."

"Can't ask you to do that," he said haltingly.

"Of course you can." She gazed down at his pinched face, watching pride war with practicality. "We're friends, remember."

"No lady ought to—"

"Save your breath—you're going to need it."

His scowl slowly quirked up into a grudging smile. "Hell's bells, I'm too weak to argue."

"A wise decision. Here, hook your arm around my shoulder..." With a few careful shifts and tugs, Harriet managed to lever his long, lanky body up from the hard ground. He had *very* broad shoulders, and as their legs touched, she was intimately aware of the chiseled planes of his thighs.

"Hmmph." Biting back a grunt, Jack swayed as he tried to shuffle his feet.

Harriet slipped a steadying hold around his waist and pretended not to notice the beads of sweat breaking out on his forehead. "Ready?"

"Aye. Lead the way."

She took a small step, then paused to reach down and grab up her reticule before continuing.

"By the by," he hissed through his clenched teeth, "what the devil do you have in there?"

"Bricks," she answered.

Jack's laugh was hardly more than a whisper, but the warmth of his breath tickled against her cheek. Amusement seemed to ripple through his limbs, the thrum reverberating against her own body.

Every bit of her skin turned rosy with the heat of him. *I'm most definitely made of flesh and blood,* she thought to herself, *not mud and water.*

"You are impossibly incorrigible."

"Which makes us birds of a feather," replied Harriet.

"So it does." After several more labored steps, he stopped to catch his breath. "How much farther do we have to fly?"

Harriet readjusted her hold around his waist, feeling the knotted tension in his back muscles. He was hurting, though she knew he would rather swallow a bayonet than admit it.

"We're almost there, thank God," she answered. "You are heavier than a sack of stones. Have you been eating more of your cousin's chocolate confections than you admit to?"

"Are you saying I am getting *fat?*"

"There does seem to be a bulge here..." She poked at the hard, flat planes of his belly. "And here."

"Minx." But as she had hoped, the barb piqued his pride just enough to spur a last spurt of strength. His stride turned steadier, and she was able to navigate the last turn and bring him around to the side gate of Lady Catherine's rear garden.

"Rafe may wax poetic on the medicinal powers of chocolate, but at the moment I would welcome a bottle of brandy," muttered Jack. "I don't suppose your friend will have any spirits stronger than ladylike sherry." He made a face. "Are you sure she won't fall into a swoon on finding a bloodied stranger at her door?"

"Quite sure. Lady Catherine is an Original. She's not easily shocked." Harriet had to struggle a bit to get him up the steps to the scullery door without a mishap. His speech was beginning to slur and she doubted he could remain upright for much longer.

Nor could she. Her jesting aside, Jack was a very big man, and all that whipcord muscle and sinew weighed far more than feathers.

"Indeed, she's likely to have a bottle of Scottish malt as well as one of brandy in her cupboard." When he didn't answer, she ventured a quick look at his face. His eyes were closed, the thick fringe of lashes black as India ink against the pale-as-a-ghost pallor of his skin.

Propping him up against one of the stone columns framing the doorway, she gave a hurried rap against the dark oak.

To her relief, Lady Catherine appeared right behind the footman who opened the door. "I'm so sorry, but there has been an accident, and I need your help—"

Her friend was already moving to grasp Jack's arm. "Let us get the gentleman inside."

BROUGHT BACK from a hazy half-consciousness by the sharp pain in his side, Jack slowly opened his eyes. "Ouch."

"Sorry," said Harriet. She rinsed the red-tinged sponge in a basin of hot water and began applying an herb-scented ointment to his ribs. "I'm almost done."

"Ye God, Harry." He stared in embarrassment at the puckered red saber scar that cut down his breastbone. "You shouldn't be exposed to this ugliness."

"I've seen a man's bare chest before," she replied as she pressed a padding of cotton wool to the knife wound. "Yours is nicer than most."

"It's a hideous disfigurement."

"It's a badge of honor," she said softly. "Now shift a bit, so I can secure the bandage."

That Harriet, who never shied away from speaking her mind, did not seem disgusted by the unsightly flaw made him feel a little less self-conscious. She was one of the very few people whose opinions he truly valued, no matter how forceful or irritating they might be. That was, he realized, because he trusted her honesty, her integrity.

"A little sticking plaster should do," said Jack gruffly. "You're a dab hand at patching up a fellow. I hardly feel a twinge."

"I think that has more to do with Lady Catherine's brandy rather than my handiwork," said Harriet dryly. "I'm happy to see it's brought a bit of color back to your face. For a few moments back there on the street, you were looking pale as a ghost."

"Having survived a saber slash, I've no intention of letting a mere knife prick cause me to stick my spoon in the wall."

"Perhaps you ought to have another swallow." She refilled the glass and held it to his lips. "This may hurt a trifle. I need to wrap the linen rather tightly to make sure the bleeding doesn't start again."

Closing his eyes, Jack relaxed against the pillows, letting the mellow warmth spread through his limbs. "No need to fuss so," he murmured, though in truth, her touch was pleasantly soothing as she went about the task.

A tug tightened the bandage around his ribs. "Right-o. I should have left you lying half dead in the alleyway."

He gave a half smile. "The devil seems half inclined to keep tossing me back to the land of the living."

"Don't keep tempting him," she scolded.

Jack repressed a yawn. He had every intention of rising and returning home, so that he could begin puzzling out how things had taken such a dangerous turn. But at present, he was feeling strangely loath to move a muscle.

Harriet finished tying the bandage and snipped off the ends. "Speaking of playing with fire, it would seem your investigation is stirring some sparks. Red Lion Square is a rougher area than Mayfair, but I've yet to hear of footpads trying to murder a gentleman, not even under the midnight shroud of darkness."

"A chance accident. They were after my purse, and I must have made them panic by fighting back so hard."

She made a rude sound. "Don't try to gammon me with such nonsense. Those men were after your life, not your money. I saw the man's face when he raised his knife."

"Damnation, you should never have—"

"We are talking about *you* at the moment, not *me*," interrupted Harriet.

"No, we are not," growled Jack. "For I have nothing more to say on the matter."

Metal clinked against metal as she tidied up the basin and tray of implements. "That is perhaps the most patronizing statement you've ever made to me." Equal measures of anger and hurt seemed to pool in her eyes. "I think I've earned better than that."

The warmth of the brandy turned to a guilty burn. "I suppose I should have known you are too sharp to be put off with platitudes about chance and fate," he conceded. "But the truth..." Jack shook his head. "I don't yet know what that is. So far, it's naught but a hellishly complicated puzzle."

"Perhaps if you trusted me with all the pieces, I could help you put it together. You seem to be... fumbling in the dark," said Harriet softly. "And that's dangerous."

Trust. Like the truth, it could be a two-edged sword. But if ever there was a person he trusted, it was Harriet.

"I admit that I haven't told you everything." Jack found the glass on the table and took another swallow. "Yes, my friend is missing, but the only reason I know of it is because his wife has secretly come here to England to find out why he seems to have disappeared." More brandy, which helped to loosen his tongue. "Camille fears that the Royalists may be involved."

"Why?" demanded Harriet.

"Apparently, Pierre is an aristocrat by birth and they feel he has betrayed his heritage."

"But why risk undertaking such a petty, personal act of

revenge when they are involved in important negotiations with our government to win a greater voice in what happens to France when Napoleon is ousted?" she responded with her usual sharp logic. "It makes no sense. If any scandal or dissent within the émigré community were to be made public, it would ruin all their hopes. Surely their leaders are smart enough to recognize that."

It was an astute observation—Jack had been thinking much the same thing. "I know, I know," he replied softly. "Her tale does have some questionable assumptions. But she's upset and frightened, so I must make allowances for that."

Harriet's brows angled to a skeptical title.

"I know what you are going to say," he hurried on. "But you don't understand. Camille drew me out of the darkest pit of despair after I thought Rafe had been killed. I'd given up on life, and she somehow managed to rekindle a spark. I owe her..." His grip tightened around the brandy glass. "I owe her the same sort of stalwart friendship, now that she's in trouble."

Harriet's only response was to start rewinding the extra length of bandage into a neat ball.

Jack shifted uncomfortably, suddenly aware that her opinion meant more to him that he cared to admit. "Well?" he finally murmured. "It's unlike you to remain silent."

"I can, on occasion, exercise tact and restraint."

He gave a wry grimace. "I'd rather you be your usual outspoken self."

"You wish to know what I really think?" she asked, not looking up from the linen.

"Your words may cut deeper than the cursed knife prick, but yes, regardless of their edge, I would like to hear them."

Harriet took her time in setting the fabric aside. "I fear you've gotten yourself into a dangerous coil. And you're thinking not with your head, but with another less rational part of your anatomy."

Jack wanted to retort, but no clever quip came to mind.

"It's clear as crystal—you love this Camille," she went on slowly.

Do I? The fact that he hesitated in answering confused him. Love should be a passionate feeling, not an intellectual conundrum.

"I thought perhaps I did," mumbled Jack. "But now..." He narrowed his eyes, watching the candlelight flicker and dance over her upswept hair. How was it that he had so rarely noticed that the simple shade of chestnut brown was in fact made up of an infinite range of nuanced highlights, ranging from bronze-dark gold to flame-tinged red.

"But now," he repeated, "my head is all a jumble."

"Understandable so," said Harriet. "Let us hope that a good night's rest will put it all to rights." Her tone, however, betrayed her skepticism.

Pressing his fingertips to his temples, Jack tried to order his thoughts. "You don't understand. Camille is sweetness and light, and all that is good. If you met her, you would see that."

"Perhaps. But as you know, I tend to think the worst of people. That way I am rarely disappointed."

"You would like her," insisted Jack.

"Let me ask you something," said Harriet, abruptly sidestepping the challenge. "Was it Camille that you met with this evening?"

"Yes," he answered tightly. "But if you are implying..." For some reason, the pounding inside his head was growing more fierce. "Damnation Harry, there are a great many possible explanations for why I was attacked. Camille could have been followed... or Amirault may have his own nefarious reasons for not wanting me looking too closely at Royalist activities... or—"

"Or Camille may have lured you to a rendezvous," said Harriet softly.

"That's absurd!" He tried to sound outraged but couldn't

muster any force behind his words. "We met by chance, and at first she tried very hard to keep me from becoming involved."

"Did she?"

He sucked in a sharp breath, sending a stab of pain through his wound. "But why?" he demanded, as much of himself as of Harriet. "Why would she wish to harm me?"

"I haven't a clue," responded Harriet. "That is what we must discover."

Jack meant to protest, but the brandy seemed to have risen in a vaporous swirl to befog his brain. How else to explain why the idea of having Harriet's help suddenly eased the ache in his chest?

He eased himself up against the pillows, shielded his eyes against the flickering candlelight and searched through the swaying shadows. "My coat—need my coat," he muttered. "Must be getting home. Much to do."

"There is," agreed Harriet as she steadied his shoulder and refastened the top two buttons of his shirt. "But I'd rather not have to scrape you up off the street for a second time tonight, so instead of trying to limp across London on your own, come with me. I've sent word for my maid and John Coachman to bring the carriage around to the alleyway skirting the back of Lady Catherine's townhouse. We should be able to take our leave without attracting undo notice."

"Let us hope no one recognized you earlier," he began.

"They didn't," she replied quickly, gathering up her pelisse and reticule. "However, if we don't hurry now, Bailin will ring a peal over my head and demand answers that I'd rather not give him."

"Just say I delayed you with some of my usual devil-may-care mischief," said Jack. He stood up gingerly, grateful to find his legs were only a trifle wobbly. "He'll have no trouble believing it."

"That solves the immediate problem. As for the bigger quandary..." Harriet looped a supporting arm around his waist and guided him toward the door. "I've not quite finished with your documents, but I hope to have the final pieces of the puzzle put together by tomorrow."

"Are you attending Lady Marquand's ball?"

"Yes." She hesitated. "But—"

"Excellent. I shall meet you there to go over your findings. I have a feeling that Pierre's whereabouts are the key to unlocking this conundrum."

"You ought not to overexert yourself by coming to a ball," she advised as they shuffled down a corridor leading to the rear entrance of the townhouse.

"I don't intend to dance," he replied. "For that matter, nor do you. So we shall have ample opportunity to find a quiet alcove and go over your notes."

"I am not sure that is wise."

"Reading," he pointed out, "doesn't qualify as a strenuous activity."

Her eyes remained locked straight ahead. Instead of answering, she merely said, "This way." The passageway narrowed and led into a small scullery. "Thank goodness Lady Catherine is very experienced in arranging discreet comings and goings from her residence. The footpath to the alleyway is shaded from curious eyes by a high yew hedge. If we hurry, we should make it to the carriage unobserved."

The oblique reminder that tittle-tattle could ruin a lady's reputation caused his steps to falter.

"Ye Gods, Harry," It suddenly struck him how egregiously self-absorbed he had been. With all the unsettling questions concerning the attack and Camille spinning around inside his head, he hadn't given a proper thought to the risks Harriet had taken for him.

Pivoting in a half-turn, he blocked the way between the two large copper wash cauldrons. "You put yourself in mortal peril tonight because of me."

It was too dark to see her face, but he felt her muscles tense. "It was not *my* liver that miscreant was trying to carve out."

"Aye, it was mine." Jack shifted again, bringing their bodies closer. "But thanks to your bravery and your bag of bricks—or whatever weighty objects were inside it—I survived."

"Numbskull though you may be at times, Kyra and Rafael seem awfully fond of you." She backed up a step, only to find the high-sided cauldron cutting off her retreat. "They would have been upset had I allowed you to be turned into *foie gras*."

He mimicked her move, slightly amused by her skittishness. "I'm grateful that you have such deadly aim."

"I've had plenty of practice," responded Harriet. "How many apples have I hurled at your head over the years?"

"Too many to count." Jack set his palms on her shoulders and leaned in closer. The gloom seemed to accentuate the subtle fragrance of her perfume. It was sweetly alluring—a unique blend of sun-kissed verbena shaded with the tang of woodland herbs.

"T-then let us not bother trying." Her whisper sounded oddly shrill. "We really must be going."

"In a moment." He stood still, simply savoring her scent and the thud of her heartbeat against his chest. Her body seemed to fit perfectly against his.

"J-Jack..." The *thump-thump* seemed to quicken to an erratic gallop.

She was nervous, and rightly so. There was still the danger of being spotted, and yet he was strangely loath to let her go. "We'll be off in a trice. But first..." He pressed his lips lightly to her brow. "I just want to say a proper thank you."

A tiny tremor shuddered through her. "What, and ruin your devil-may-care reputation?" Wriggling sideways, she slipped free of his hold and grabbed his sleeve. "Fine, fine—I shall consider myself thanked. Now come along."

CHAPTER 10

"Ooooh, Miss Harriet, I vow, you look more beautiful than those fancy ladies in Ackermann's fashion plates."

"Do I?" Forcing her gaze back to the cheval glass, Harriet blinked several times to clear her focus. Her thoughts had been wrapped up in brooding over Jack and his fleeting kiss—if a kiss it had been. She still wasn't sure what to call it.

"La, just look at the way those lovely ringlets frame your face!" exclaimed Ellie, after twitching a ribbon into place and stepping back to and admire the effect. "Monsieur Etienne is a true artist with his scissors."

Earlier in the day, Mrs. Currough had sent over one of her *haute monde* friends to fashion a new hairstyle for both her and Theo. Now, as Harriet contemplated her reflection, she found herself admitting the effect wasn't half-bad. The fellow had made a show of studying their faces and had been quite restrained with his snipping.

She turned her head one way and then the other. It was quite striking how just a subtle change could make her look so different. The shape of her cheeks, the line of her jaw, the width of her mouth—her face appeared transformed.

"I feel more elegant," she murmured. "Which is of course absurd. I'm still the same old Harriet."

"Ha!" Ellie carefully fluffed out the gossamer-light overskirt of her ball gown and let out a dreamy sigh. "You're like a cygnet in one of those fairie stories you read to me—you know, who magically turns into a beautiful swan."

"Magic, indeed." Harriet smoothed her hands over her hips, sure that no mere mortal could spin silk so soft and fine. "Let us hope that at midnight I don't find myself transformed into a turnip."

"You and Lady Theo are going to be the belles of the ball," assured her maid.

A glance at the mantel clock showed that she had best be on her way. She had promised to have her carriage stop for Theo and her mother, so that they could arrive together.

It was, as Jack had often told her, important to have moral support when charging into battle. Camaraderie might not stop bullets, but it helped to calm jumpy nerves.

Already her heart was ricocheting off her ribcage. And the thought of Jack made the hammering even more pronounced.

What if he thinks me foolish?

"Then he can go to the devil," she murmured, trying to buck up her courage.

"What was that?" Ellie turned from taking a Kashmir shawl from the armoire.

"Nothing," answered Harriet as she took up the notes from her desk and stuffed them into the matching jade green reticule.

Her maid made a pained face. "You ought to take the smaller one." She had fallen in love with a delicate shell-shaped creation that hung from the wrist by a silver cord.

"Fashion must give way to practicality."

"That's not very romantic," muttered Ellie under her breath.

"Which suits me just fine." After slanting one last glance at the looking glass, Harriet headed for the stairs, reminding herself to glide, not stomp.

The carriage ride was a short one, and before she had quite prepared herself for swanning through the glare of glittering torchlight, it was time to descend and join the crowd of ladies in jewel-spangled gowns and gentlemen in dark evening dress making their way up the circular staircase.

Theo's mother had stopped in the cavernous entrance hall to gossip with several of her cronies, leaving the two young ladies to head on to the ballroom on their own.

"People are staring at us," whispered Theo, after casting a furtive look around.

Harriet made a wry face. "They are probably trying to figure out who we are."

Sure enough, Lady Jerrett, one of the highest sticklers of society despite her penchant for wearing purple turbans festooned with peacock plumes, swiveled her ample bulk and raised a gold lorgnette to her narrowed eyes. The scrutiny lasted several long moments before her brows winged up in surprise.

"Miss Farnum." A pause. "You are looking... well." The lenses shifted to Theo and Lady Jerrett's expression became even more perplexed. "I daresay I almost didn't recognize you, Lady Theo." Another owlish squint. "Er, are those gowns by Madame Deauville?"

Several of the other ladies nearby stopped chatting and waited expectantly.

"Yes," replied Harriet, arching a cool smile. "They are."

"I wasn't aware that you were clients. She has a *very* small list." After making a few mental calculations, Lady Jerrett gave a tiny nod. "I am having a small soiree next week. I shall send around an invitation to you gels." To her companion, she added, "The bucks of the *ton* are more apt to show up if they hear there will be a bevy of beauties in attendance."

Theo looked a little stunned as the matron moved up the stairs. "W-we are beauties?"

Harriet didn't know how to answer. She, too, was unused to garnering a second glance from society's arbiters of style. Squaring her shoulders, she straightened her spine and lifted her chin. "Let us not forget our lessons," she counseled in a low murmur. "Just follow my lead. Beautiful or not in the flesh, we can at least appear regal and graceful."

His evening shoes beating an impatient tattoo on the cobbles, Jack crossed the street and hurried through the elegant colonnaded portal. A mood of merriment was already echoing off the marble walls of the hall, the overloud voices punctuated by trilling laughter and the soft fizz of champagne.

He skirted around the milling couples and took the stairs two at a time. Harriet, he knew, would not be lingering downstairs in the crush of guests. His mouth quirked, thinking of her standing in her usual quiet spot in the shadows, observing the festivities. Given her razor-sharp eye—and razor sharp sense of the absurd —it was no wonder she was such a keen judge of character.

Taking a glass of champagne from the servant stationed on the landing, Jack was just about to pass through the ballroom's arched entryway when he spotted James standing in the foyer of the card room.

"What are you doing skulking in the shadows?" he asked.

"Thinking." James quaffed a long swallow of his wine.

"Ye Gods, that explains the blue-deviled phiz," quipped Jack. "You're a frivolous fribble. You never think."

"I am now."

He signaled to a passing waiter to refill his friend's glass. "Have you seen Harry? She and Lady Theo were planning on arriving together."

James's face went through a series of odd little contortions. "Yes."

"And?" he pressed.

"You'll see," was the only response.

"Are you perchance foxed?"

"No." His friend drained his drink. "But I plan to be rather quickly."

"What the devil is wrong?" he demanded. "You're making even less sense than usual."

"You'll see," repeated James darkly, casting a jerky glance at the ballroom.

Deciding it was futile trying to pry out any further information, given his friend's current unfathomable mood, Jack cocked a mock salute and stalked off.

"Arse," he muttered under his breath. But try as he might, he couldn't quite quell the frisson of unease stirred by the encounter.

The dancing had begun, setting the room ablaze with swirls of richly-colored silks and the diamond-bright flashes of fire from the overhead chandeliers. Craning his neck, Jack made a sweeping search of the side alcoves, only to see naught but the swaying, dark-fingered fronds of the potted palms.

Damnation, where was she? He turned abruptly to check the far end of the room—and froze in mid-step as his gaze fell on a laughing lady spinning by in the arms of a well-known Corinthian.

Theo? He blinked, wondering whether the dipping, darting light was playing tricks with his eyes. But no, the couple circled around again, and this time there was no mistaking his friend. Their eyes locked for an instant, and she flashed a wry smile before being swallowed in the whirling dervish blur of couples.

Now thoroughly off-balance, Jack retreated to a recessed alcove in the colonnade. Brows drawing together, he sipped pensively at his champagne. His expectations for the evening seemed to be unraveling in a hurry...

Another flutter of silk stirred in the shadows nearby and suddenly the effervescence of the wine felt like dagger points dancing over his tongue.

Her upswept hair threaded in luminous pearls, her voluptuous body swathed in a pale sky-blue hue that matched her eyes, Camille was a vision of ethereal loveliness. For an instant, he couldn't breathe, but the spell gave way to an urgent question.

What was she doing here?

Setting aside his glass, he moved around quietly to approach her from an oblique angle. As he came closer, he saw she was engaged in earnest conversation with another fashionable lady, whose dark hair and emerald green gown were a striking counterpoint to Camille's pastel beauty.

Dark and Light.

Jack paused to watch them, wondering why he hadn't ever noticed the fox-like glitter of Camille's eyes. Vixen-bright, they seemed to be ever alert, as if constantly on the hunt for some vulnerable prey. He quickly shook off the ungracious thought, reminding himself that this was the woman who had drawn him back from the brink of hell. He was still unsettled by the recent attack. Harriet had planted some unwelcome suggestions, and try as he might, he couldn't dismiss them out of hand.

Harriet. As a flicker of light penetrated the gloom and lit the coppery highlights in the dark-haired lady's tresses, the penny finally dropped.

Swallowing his shock, Jack forced himself forward.

On hearing his steps, the two ladies turned as one.

"Ah, there you are, sir."

Yes, the voice was definitely that of Harriet. As for the rest of her...

"I was just informing your friend that you were expected to put in an appearance," finished Harriet, flashing him a peculiar look. He didn't have time to decipher its meaning because at the same time, Camille saw him, and gave a theatrical little sway as she placed a hand on her breast.

"Jac-ques!" she exclaimed, drawing out the two French-sounding syllables like a length of warm toffee. "I did not expect to see you here."

And why is that? he wondered.

"But your *amie*, Mademoiselle Farnum, was just telling me that since your return to England, you have grown very fond of the glitter and gaiety of the social whirl."

"I was saying no such thing," corrected Harriet. "I simply mentioned that you occasionally attend parties."

"When he lay wounded in our house, Jack confided in me that he didn't like the superficial trappings of society," said Camille. Turning to him, she smiled. "*N'est pas,* Jack?"

Harriet was watching the other woman intently. Jack thought he detected a tiny twitch of ironic humor tug at the corners of her mouth and felt himself flush, though he wasn't quite sure why.

"I think you may rest assured that his sentiments haven't changed, Madame La Rochelle," said Harriet softly.

"Oh?" Camille shot her a probing look. "It sounds as if the two of you know each other well."

"Well enough," replied Harriet, giving nothing away.

Jack dragged his eyes away from her. A myriad of questions were spinning inside his head, but he shoved them aside until later. At the moment he was determined to concentrate on Camille.

Was it simply his imagination, or was there some new sly and guarded nuance shading the Frenchwoman's face? Harriet, he had noted, was getting better at masking her feelings—a fact he wasn't sure he liked—but whatever her expression, there was no hint of guile.

"Then we have something in common, Mademoiselle

Farnum," said Camille, drawing him back from his momentary brooding. "For I daresay Jack and I know each other well enough, too." The curl of her lashes hid all but a few hide-and-seek shimmers of blue. "Our time together may have been short, but the shared dangers in wartime tend to strengthen the bond of friendship in ways that may be difficult for others to comprehend."

A half step angled her body closer to his—a small but intimate move that seemed to distance the two of them from Harriet.

"All of Jack's friends here in England are very grateful to you and your husband for bringing him back from the dead."

"And you, Miss Farnum?" asked Camille with a light laugh. "Could it be that you have a special tendre for him?"

"One tends to have trouble feeling a tendre for the imp of Satan who put a great ugly toad in her sewing basket when she was twelve," murmured Harriet in reply.

"It was a frog," murmured Jack. "Perhaps if you had kissed it, the slippery little devil would have turned into a prince."

"My lips were too busy cursing you from here to Hades," she shot back.

He repressed a grin. "Your knowledge of invectives would put a stevedore to blush."

"I have never claimed to be a proper lady."

Camille was following the exchanges with great interest. "*Non?* I thought all young English misses are taught to be paragons of propriety." A flick of her finger brushed an errant curl from her cheek. "While we French seem to have a penchant for rebelling against the rules."

"An interesting observation," said Harriet. "Though I've always felt it's unwise to make such generalizations."

Jack noted the quicksilver ripple of annoyance that flitted across Camille's features. "You are right, of course. I am not always wise." Her eyes found his. "Like many who possess the Gallic temperament, I am too often ruled by my passions."

Swirling beneath the shimmering blue was an elemental

appeal, all the more intimate for being unspoken. It seemed to wrap around his consciousness, a tantalizingly soft and alluring reminder that life and death had irrevocably entwined them.

The sound of approaching steps broke the connection before he had to respond.

"Ah, here you are, Madame La Rochelle. I feared you might be feeling overwhelmed by the crush of strangers, but it seems you have found company."

"Jac—that is, Lord Leete—and I are old friends."

"Indeed?" Amirault gave no acknowledgment of Harriet's presence. "I wasn't aware that the two of you were acquainted."

Jack sensed it was a bald-faced lie but schooled his expression to a bland smile. "I met Madame and her husband while I was a prisoner of war."

"Ah, how ironic. For now, it seems the situation is reversed."

"Monsieur le Comte has kindly offered to see if he might discover some news of Pierre," explained Camille in a tight whisper.

"I thought you did not wish to make official inquiries," said Jack.

"My inquiries will not be made through any of your tedious government departments," replied Amirault. "I have my own network for seeking the information that Madame La Rochelle desires."

"Let us hope they can be trusted to be discreet," said Harriet. "Madame was telling me earlier that she is concerned that there are some unknown forces who may wish her husband harm."

Amirault turned. "Miss Farnum." His voice held a note of surprise. "Forgive me, I did not recognize you standing there in the shadows." His gaze slowly moved from her face to the creamy expanse of flesh exposed by her fashionably-cut bodice—and lingered there long enough that Jack itched to plant him a facer.

"I applaud your sense of style," he said. "Madame Deauville is a gifted modiste. You are fortunate to be among the select few she consents to dress."

"So I am told," replied Harriet.

"Might I inquire how you came to be in her good graces?" he asked.

"Oh, come, a lady likes to have her little secrets."

Recalling her recent comments about wishing to be mysterious, Jack had to concede that Harriet was doing a good job of it. *Too good, in fact.* He was wondering much the same thing. It was one thing to purchase a shawl at Madame Deauville's shop, but quite another to have the famous modiste consent to fashion a ballgown.

But before he could ponder the question any further, Camille slipped a hand around his arm and drew him aside.

"Please don't be angry with me, *cheri*," she whispered. "There are things that I can't explain right now, save to say that we French sometimes use different methods than you English for achieving our goals."

"But at what cost, Camille?" he responded.

She looked away. "I don't expect you to understand. But I hope with all my heart that it won't affect our friendship."

Friendship, he wanted to point out, was built on honesty and trust. And yet he held his tongue, waiting to see what else she might say.

"Alors, I can sense you are truly upset."

Jack wasn't precisely sure how to describe his emotions. But at that instant, he was aware of a fundamental shift happening somewhere deep inside him.

"You must, of course, do what you think is best for you and Pierre," he answered politely.

"Thank you for that, *cheri*." She smiled, but her gaze grew opaque, shutting him out. Or perhaps it had never been quite so open as he had imagined.

The silence was kept from growing too awkward by Amirault,

who chose that moment to finish his tête-á-tête with Harriet. "Loathe though I am to break up this congenial group, there are several people I wish for Madame La Rochelle to meet." He extended his hand to Camille. "So if you would kindly excuse us."

Jack was not unhappy to see him go, especially as the Comte paused for a last glance at Harriet. "I look forward to conversing again soon, Miss Farnum. It seems we share a number of interests."

He waited, holding his temper in check, until the couple had moved out of earshot. "Don't trust that bloody hypocrite," he growled through clenched teeth. "I hope you are smart enough to see he merely wants to use you for his own ends." His brows pinched together as he added, "Whatever they may be."

CHAPTER 11

"I am not a complete ninnyhammer," said Harriet, still watching the sensuous sway of Camille's hips as the French lady and Amirault strolled through the crowd and disappeared into the card room. "Of course I realize the Comte has ulterior motives for trying to seduce his way into my good graces." The real question was whether Jack understood the import of his own warning.

"Seduce—hmmph! Had he leaned in any closer to your bodice, his nose would have been in your cleavage," he muttered gruffly. "What were you discussing?"

"The fabric and cut of my gown. Amirault, for all his faults, is very *au courant* about the latest fashions."

Another grunt.

"And," continued Harriet, "we discussed the hairstyles. He was of the opinion that the new fringe of ringlets frames my face rather nicely."

Jack looked a little nonplussed. "I..." His eyes narrowed. "I noticed that you had cut your hair. But..."

"But what?" she inquired, hoping to keep a note of disappointment from creeping into her voice. It was silly to expect a compliment from Jack. His tongue was made of razored steel, not sun-kissed honey.

"But I thought you wouldn't want me to waste time making a fuss about it." Jack shuffled his feet, as if the parquet beneath his shoes had suddenly turned to red-hot coals. "Dash it all, Harry. You've always been different than other girls. You don't need all that silly simpering over the color of a ribbon or the flutter of a flounce. You're practical and sensible—"

"In other words, very brick-like," she murmured.

"I can talk to you." He essayed a note of humor. "I can't talk to a brick. Or rather, I can, but it won't answer back with your intelligence or insight."

She heaved an inward sigh, deciding she was fighting a losing battle. In his eyes, no matter how many layers of fancy silks and frothy lace she donned, she would always be a humdrum sort of building block, useful but hardly something that sparked any deeper passion.

Intelligence and insight were not the first compliments a lady might long to hear at a fancy ball, but they would have to do.

Jack cleared his throat with a cough. "Er, speaking of intelligence and insight, did you bring your notes?"

"Yes," replied Harriet. "Much to the dismay of my maid, who thought this large reticule ruined the lines of my gown."

With naught but a wordless grunt in response, Jack retreated a step deeper into the shelter of the potted palms, taking the sheets of papers she had slipped into his hands.

She was only vaguely aware that the music was starting up for a new set of dances when a soft hail drew her attention away from Jack's pensive profile.

"Excuse me, Miss Farnum, but might I ask you to dance?"

Oh, surely Addison, the Adonis of Mayfair, wasn't asking *her* to step out with him. He was not only notoriously good-looking but also notoriously choosy in whom he deigned to lead out on the dance floor.

Harriet drew in her breath to answer—

"Go away, Addison," snapped Jack.

"My apologies, Leete. I didn't realize you and the lady were engaged for this gavotte." To Harriet, he added politely, "Then may I get in line for the next one."

"She's taken for that as well. Now run along and stop pestering us."

Addison opened his mouth to speak, but on catching Jack's scowl he seemed to think better of it and backed off without a word.

"That," she huffed, "was exceedingly rude."

Paper crackled as he turned a page. "He's a pompous bore."

"Be that as it may, how did you know whether or not I wanted to dance?"

"Do you?"

Harriet looked longingly at the couples twirling across the polished parquet, their laughter twining with the capering melody of the violins. She thought of her beautiful gown and how, in the privacy of her room, she had spun round and round in front of the cheval glass, marveling at how the gossamer silk had floated in soft, sensuous, lighter-than-air undulations.

"Yes, as a matter of fact, I do."

When he merely went back to reading, she was sorely tempted to stamp her foot in frustration—that, or aim a swift kick at his lordly posterior.

Wretch. That he seemed oblivious to the wiles of Camille made her even more furious. Fine—let him be ensnared by her sultry charms. If he insisted on playing the fool, it was none of her business. She had done her part in piecing together his dratted puzzle. Now he was on his own.

Looking around, Harriet felt a rush of relief on spotting Theo at the refreshment table.

"Excuse me, I shall be back shortly." Without waiting for a response, she lifted her skirts and glided off, though it took all of her self-control to keep from stomping her delicate, ribbon-trimmed dancing shoes loud enough to wake the Devil.

~

"HAVE SOME CHAMPAGNE." James pushed through the palm fronds. "I am tired of drinking alone."

Thrusting the papers, inside his coat, Jack accepted the wine. The crystal was cool against his fingers, and the sparkling fizz of the tiny bubbles stirred the sudden realization of how thirsty he was.

"A toast," muttered James, clumsily clinking glass to glass. "May a great gaping hole open up in the middle of the dance floor and swallow all the prowling peacocks."

"Peacocks don't prowl," scoffed Jack before letting a mouthful of the pale gold liquid course down his throat.

"Ha!" James cocked a nod at the refreshment table. "Take a look for yourself."

A sputtering choke set the leaves to chattering. "What the devil are they doing?"

"Do you mean 'they' as in Theo and Harriet, or 'they' as in all the fribbles and jackanapes buzzing around their skirts?"

Jack squinted through the greenery. "Both."

"The ladies are merely looking... magnificently alluring. While the gentlemen are making cakes of themselves with all their outrageous flirting and flatteries."

"Damnation," growled Jack.

"Damnation," echoed James, as he drained his glass and slumped a shoulder against the wall. "Did you notice their gowns?"

"Yes," muttered Jack. "I noticed."

"S'not right. All those fellows drawn to the fancy new clothes and the..." James paused. "No, it's not just the clothes, lovely as they are. It's more than that." Looking thoroughly bewildered, he grimaced and shook his head. "Though I can't for the life of me say what it is."

Jack watched the men flitting around Harriet and Theo, dark moths drawn to the firebright flame of their allure. He couldn't quite articulate it either. "It's as if by some perverse magic, Harriet and Theo suddenly came to see themselves differently—and now, so do all the bucks of the *ton* who never gave them a second glance."

"Aye," agreed James glumly. "Those fellows see the outward elegance and grace but they don't know the real essence of our ladies. How they are thoughtful and easy to talk to, how they are kind and compassionate, how they have a sly sense of humor."

Jack regarded his friend with a quizzical stare. "You do realize that you are thoroughly cupshot."

"Yes." James slid a few inches lower on the wall. "Not making any sense, I know. So I think I shall toddle off to the street... and puke on cobbles rather than on one of Lady Henning's priceless Aubusson carpets."

Jack offered a steadying hand, but James waved him off. "S'all right. Can see m'self out. In no mood for company."

As his friend staggered away, Jack angled another glowering look at the crowd around the punch bowl, where it seemed every man in the room was busy drinking in the sight of Harriet and Theo sipping their champagne. James, for all his wine-garbled babbling, had hit upon the essence of the matter. All the other men only saw the outer glitter, not the inner gold.

He blinked, and all of a sudden had to lean back and brace himself against the sliver of wall James had just vacated.

Ye Gods, how long had he been blind to the truth?

How had he ever imagined that he might be in love with Camille? Her allure was like a curl of smoke. There was a certain fascination to its undulating beauty, but in the end, it was no more substantial than a puff of vapor. While Harriet was a like a blade of sunlight, strong, substantial and radiant with warmth.

She pushed, provoked him, and infuriated him, all the while challenging him to be more than he thought he could be.

He wasn't sure he was capable of love and all its emotional complexities, but friendship was perhaps even more elemental.

Jack drew in a measured breath, trying to figure out just when it had happened. Impossible to pin down the exact moment when Harriet had crept under his defenses, under his skin and become a touchstone, a way of keeping hold of the better part of his nature. The bond of friendship—the trust, the laughter, the sharing of thoughts—now felt so natural that he couldn't imagine himself without it.

Placing his glass in one of the terra cotta pots, Jack pushed his way free of the shadows.

As the musicians began tuning their instruments for the opening notes of a waltz, Harriet heard Theo turn away yet another request for her hand.

"I thought you were enjoying the dancing," she murmured.

"I am," replied Theo. "I—I just don't quite feel like waltzing."

Neither do I, thought Harriet, quelling the urge to look for Jack among the swaying trees across the room.

They had moved from the refreshment table to a quieter spot near the bevy of chaperones seated by the arched windows. Yet even the proximity of the Dragons hadn't kept some of the gentlemen from following and pressing for a place on their dance cards.

"Though I confess, it is very romantic to twirl across the floor to such a lilting melody."

"That depends on your partner," pointed out Harriet, reminding herself that she was still cross as crabs with Jack.

Theo sighed and started to hum along softly under her breath.

The sound masked the light tread of steps approaching from the rear.

Which explained why she nearly jumped out of her skin when the touch of fingertip grazed against her bare shoulder.

"Sorry. But may I have a word with you?"

"Why?" she asked, turning slowly to face Jack.

In answer, he took her hand, his grip surprisingly gentle, yet firm, and drew her with quick-footed steps between two massive urns filled with roses. The heady perfume filled her nostrils, making her feel a little light-headed.

"You did say you wanted to dance," he murmured, shifting his hold. Through the butter-soft leather of his glove, she could feel the calloused contours of his palm, the tapered strength of his fingers as they slid over her hip.

"Y-yes, but I didn't say I wanted to dance with *you.*"

The smile that curled up the corners of his mouth made her heart lurch up against her ribs.

"I don't blame you. I've been acting like an arse."

Heat flared at the small of her back as his hand came to rest and pulled her closer. Their thighs touched in a rustle of wool and lace, setting off sparks that seemed to melt into the very marrow of her bones.

His hold tightened. "Are you alright?"

"It's a trifle overwarm in here." Harriet fanned her face. "I'm fine. It's passed."

Jack led her the few remaining steps to the perimeter of the dance floor. She was grateful for the intermittent shadows that hide the flush she knew was creeping to her face.

"Will you forgive me?" he asked quietly, all trace of sardonic humor gone from his voice.

"F-for what?"

"As I said, for acting like an arse."

"You have been doing that ever since I can remember." She

tipped her head and their eyes met. "But yes, we are friends, Jack. That's a bond hard to break."

"Even for an arse?" Amusement danced in his dark eyes.

She nodded, not quite trusting her voice. Her throat seemed to have tightened for no reason, and the rest of her body was reacting with strange little shivers of fire and ice.

"Then raise your arms. The dance is about to begin."

Harriet knew the proper position—one hand on his shoulder, the other lifted to fit against his palm. Intimately aware of the breadth of muscle, the contours of his shape, she pressed against him, feeling her flesh mold to his through the thin layers of fabric. She could picture all the little nuances that had come to be so familiar—the ridged scar along his knuckles, where he had cut himself helping her brother William climb down from a barn roof, the lump on his collarbone, a memento of a fall from his horse.

The sense of connection—two as one—nearly took her breath away.

Jack seemed to feel it too. A tiny tremor pulsed along the line of his jaw, and as he angled his head, the fringe of his lashes couldn't quite hide the oddly vulnerable look in his eyes. In contrast, his body moved with a confident grace, his step sure, guiding her through the first few spins.

She relaxed, letting the natural harmony of their movements match the melody of the lovely music. Her anger had long since ebbed away. However maddening his moments of sarcasm could be, it was impossible to ignore the comfortable camaraderie that lay beneath all their banter and bickering.

Friendship wasn't easy. But maybe it was easier than love.

"Still seething?"

"No." Her skirts ruffled against their legs as they glided round and round through a circling turn.

"Shall I continue guessing at your emotions? You aren't usually so quiet, so something must be holding your tongue."

"I'm simply enjoying the moment," answered Harriet.

Jack quickened his steps, the elaborate patterns turning fluid beneath their feet. "As am I. You dance very well."

She accepted his words with a smile. "A compliment from you? Have a care—I may swoon on the dance floor."

"I did notice the cut of your hair, and how the ringlets curl around the curve of your jaw and tickle the shell of your ear. Just as I noticed how the color of your gown captures the deepest hue of your eyes, and how its design makes you look light as a feather floating on a puff of sun-warmed air."

Harriet stumbled, and only his strong hands kept her from falling.

"But as I don't have Lord Byron's gift of language, I did not attempt to say so."

The thrumming in her ears was almost loud enough to drown out the music, but somehow she managed to follow along.

"So now," he went on, "I'll stop spouting nonsense and move on to far more important things."

Like his feelings for Camille?

Swallowing the lump in her throat, Harriet said, "You may not wish to hear it, but before we do so, I too, have a word of warning."

"You wish to point out that Madame La Rochelle may be using me for her own ends."

"It seems a possibility," she answered carefully.

For an instant, it appeared his attention was focused on some far-off spot in the room. Then his gaze came back to their twined hands, bright in the crystalline flicker of candle-light. "Like you, I am not blind to the wiles of my French friend."

A knot seemed to loosen in her chest, and suddenly it was easier to breathe.

"If all this talk about Pierre's disappearance is an elaborate farriddiddle," he added, "then the question is why?"

"Why, indeed," Harriet mused. "Does it matter? You could simply walk away."

"I'm a stubborn fellow. I don't like leaving conundrums unsolved." Another graceful spin, though she was aware of his muscles hardening. "Especially when they involve a betrayal of loyalties. Something havey-cavey is afoot, and now that I've been drawn into the mystery, I mean to learn what it is. But you need not feel compelled to help any longer. You've done enough already—"

"Of course I'm going to help," she cut in. "I'm just as stubborn as you are. Maybe more so."

A grin slowly softened the taut planes of his face. "I was hoping you might say that. Your counsel and camaraderie would be most welcome."

"There's just one thing I need you to answer honestly, Jack. Are you in love with Camille La Rochelle? It will affect how we hunt for the truth, and I'd rather know now if it will be an issue."

"No." His answer came softly yet swiftly, without a hint of hesitation. "I've come to realize she never really touched my heart."

Harriet wanted to ask how he knew, but before she could frame the question, his next words drove the thought from her head.

"But the fact is, I'm not sure I'm capable of loving anyone, seeing as I don't much like myself."

Their hands were pressed palm to palm, and she slowly curled her fingers, entwining them with his. Warmth pulsed between them as she gave a small squeeze. "Why?"

The question seemed to take him by surprise, and for several long moments, she thought he didn't mean to answer. But then it was her turn to hear something unexpected.

"At times," Jack said, "I feel like a rudderless ship, at the mercy of the buffeting winds and swirling currents when storms arise, rather than able to steer my own course."

"Where do you want to go?" asked Harriet quietly.

"Ah, there have been a great many questions asked tonight, but precious few answers have sounded in return."

Harriet refused to be diverted. "Yes, answers are hard to find. But if you put your hand on the tiller, and choose a direction to follow, you may surprise yourself."

"You make it sound easy," said Jack.

"It isn't. But if you believe in yourself, anything is possible." She paused. "Look at me, and Theo. We thought it beyond the realm of imagination that we might ever learn the art of appearing poised and graceful. However, several wise acquaintances counseled us that the first lesson was to believe we could do it. And lo and behold, we are, I think, making a little headway."

"So *that* is the magic," he murmured.

"No witches or warlocks, no potions or spells."

A noiseless laugh ruffled her curls. He said nothing more, but tucked her closer and whirled through a set of spins that left her a little dizzy.

Or maybe it was the scent of him—the light fragrance of bay rum, starch and some earthy, elementally male essence—that was overpowering her sense.

Somehow, Harriet kept her feet moving, moving...

"Jack."

"Hmm?" His lips were close, so the sound feathered against her ear. But for some reason, he sounded as if he were very far away.

"The music has stopped."

"Has it?" He slowed to a stop, and yet his body still seemed to be thrumming with some silent arpeggio only he could hear.

"*Jack,*" she hissed, trying to slip free from his hold. People were beginning to stare.

He opened his eyes. "Damnation, the music has stopped. And we still have a battle plan to draw up."

"Perhaps that ought to wait until tomorrow." Harriet was not confident that she could think straight at the present moment.

"You may be right." Jack finally roused himself to escort her off the dance floor. "I shall come around to your townhouse in the early afternoon. We can take a stroll through Green Park, which will afford plenty of privacy for discussing plans. There were several points in your notes that bear further thought."

"I have a better idea," she replied. "Let us visit the new painting exhibit at the Royal Academy."

He frowned. "There will likely to be a crowd."

"Yes, and among the visitors will be Amirault. He told me so earlier tonight."

"Harry, I would rather you stay away from him."

"Oh, come. The fact that Camille turned to him can't be coincidence."

His jaw tightened.

"It's key that we learn what they are up to, and I'm the one who can do that. Both of them were asking some very pointed questions about my father. If I play along with their game, I'll be in a position to uncover some answers of my own."

"You didn't mention the queries," said Jack, looking unhappy at her revelations.

"I—I didn't have a chance."

"If we are to do this together, we cannot have secrets from each other," he insisted.

"I agree," answered Harriet. But inwardly she feared that despite their best intentions, the secrets within secrets might take on a life of their own.

CHAPTER 12

"Well, well, if it isn't Lothario," quipped Sir Lucas Whalley, who was seated by the fireplace of the reading room at White's.

Jack shot the fellow a quelling look as he paused in the doorway and handed his coat to one of the club's hall porters.

"I thought you claimed to have no interest in innocents, as you're adamant about not sticking your paw in the parson's mousetrap," chimed in a ginger-whiskered baron whom Jack recognized from their Oxford days.

Lord Addison lowered his newspaper and peered down his aristocratic nose. "And yet you sent me away with a flea in my ear when I tried to dance with the lovely Miss Farnum. That's not playing fair, Leete. Just because you have no romantic designs on the season's most eligible young ladies, doesn't mean you should prevent the rest of us from striking up a flirtation."

"Harriet doesn't like to flirt," growled Jack, in no mood for needling. He had come to his club to meet James and have a hearty breakfast, not trade barbs with his fellow members on an empty stomach.

"If your scowl is anywhere near as black as it is now," retorted Addison, "It's no wonder."

"Ha, ha, ha," chortled the others.

"But then," added Addison with a sly grin. "Perhaps a French saber isn't the only thing that has pierced your hide. Perhaps Cupid's arrow has found its mark. A good many guests noticed how you appeared glued to Miss Farnum's skirts."

"And very lovely skirts they were," noted Whalley.

"Put a cork in it," snapped Jack. "Unless you want to be digging your front teeth out of your gullet."

"Oooh, a bit touchy, are we?" teased Ginger-Whiskers. "I think you may be right, Addy. The arrow may have struck his heart." He clasped a hand to his chest and gave an exaggerated grimace. "Leete may be in love."

"Quite impossible," responded Jack. "I told the surgeons to leave out my heart when they stitched me back up."

More laughter, along with another few ribald comments.

Spotting James sitting in a shadowed corner, he ignored the chortles and gave an impatient wave. "Come, let us leave these bacon-brained fribbles to their witticisms and go have a bite of beefsteak. I'm famished, and I have a busy day ahead of me."

"Squiring Miss Farnum around Town?" inquired Whalley. "I say, do introduce me to her friend—Lady Theo or Thalia, or whatever her name is. I always thought of her as plump and unremarkable in looks, but recently she seems to have undergone a transformation."

"Speaking of plump, I hear her father is about to become very plump in the pocket," said Ginger-Whiskers. "Word is, he's invested in a company that owns the largest silver mine in the New World and will soon be rolling in money."

He cleared his throat. "Might as well introduce me to the gel as well. For that sort of blunt, I'd be willing to bed an antidote, but as Whalley says, she's not half bad to look at, and—Arrgh!"

A sputtering gasp cut off his words as half a bottle of brandy spilled into his lap.

"So sorry." James shrugged and stared at the man's sodden trousers with a faint smirk. "How terribly clumsy of me. Must have tripped on the carpet."

Repressing a snort, Jack followed his friend into the corridor. "Well aimed," he murmured.

"Never did like Graves. Too puffed up with a sense of his own importance." He walked on several steps. "Lady Theo wouldn't like him either."

"I daresay both Lady Theo and Harriet are too clever and smart for most of the men who belong to White's. Including us."

"We're not scheming to win their regard because of family influence or money," said James morosely.

"True," mused Jack as he chose a quiet table by the window and ordered breakfast and a pot of coffee. "Though there have been moments when I wondered—"

"No," intoned his friend, silencing the speculation with a decided shake of his head. "Absolutely not."

They slid into their seats, and after a moment it was James who broke the silence by venturing an oblique question. "There was a small bit of gossip in the newspaper this morning, referring to your obvious attention to a certain lady—"

"Purely business," assured Jack. "Nothing more."

"Well then, it seems we're both safe from a legshackle."

"Quite safe."

Silver clinked and napkins rustled as they prepared for the arrival of their food. "Speaking of business, Jamie, I was wondering whether you might consent to do me a small favor."

"Are you paying for the beefsteak?"

"I'll gladly pay for a half dozen beefsteaks."

"Excellent. I've run through my quarterly allowance, and Pater is being a nipcheese about advancing any further funds."

Eyeing the deep shadows under James's eyes and how his skin

was drawn tight over his cheekbones, Jack asked, "Do you wish to talk about why?"

"Not particularly," muttered his friend. Waving to a waiter, he ordered a flagon of ale to go along with the coffee.

Jack had heard rumors that his friend had been spending more and more time at the gaming hells around Town. But whatever devils were plaguing James, he did not feel it was wise to press him.

"So, what is this small favor?"

"I know you are fast friends with Robert Hockett, who works in the Home Office, so I was hoping you might consent to make some inquiries for me." Jack proceeded to list several questions. "Needless to say, it all needs to be done very discreetly."

James had slowly straightened from his slouch as he listened. "Interesting. You think there is something havey-cavey going on within the French émigré community?"

"Yes, but at the moment, I'd rather not go into details."

"Fair enough. Consider it done." James drank deeply of his ale. "But discretion will cost you several suppers in addition to breakfast."

The rest of the meal passed in casual talk of the upcoming horse races at Newmarket and the latest model dueling pistols displayed in Joseph Manton's shop. However, Jack began to fidget when his friend ordered a helping of eggs and gammon after polishing off his plate of beefsteak.

"Have you a rendezvous?" asked James around a mouthful of sultana muffin.

"Yes, in fact, I do." He punctuated the point by consulting his pocket watch. "I'm already late. So if you don't mind, I'll leave you to devour the rest of your breakfast... or is it now luncheon?"

"Ha, ha, ha. Shall I see you here for supper? Or shall we meet at The Devil's Pitchfork tavern?"

"You're spending enough time in the hells as it is." Jack shoved back his chair and rose. "I suggest you go home and get some sleep."

As he walked away, a low laugh sounded from the table. "No rest for the wicked."

~

HARRIET and her maid circled around through the columned archway and took another turn down the long gallery.

"People are staring," whispered Ellie approvingly. "I told you that particular walking dress is mayhap the prettiest of the lot. The burnt-gold hue suits your coloring to perfection. And that mutton-sleeved spencer is magnificent. The nipped waist and frogging make you look oh-so elegant."

"I hate to disappoint you, but I doubt they are studying my clothing," replied Harriet. Theo had sent round a note earlier in the day, warning about the bit of tittle-tattle in the morning newspaper. "More likely they are trying to gather together the threads of gossip that have recently been making the rounds." She sighed. "And stitch them into a scandal."

Her maid's eyes widened slightly. "Oh, never say you've been spotted around Red Lion Square."

"No, it has to do with last night, at Lord and Lady Henning's ball."

"Did something scandalous happen?" asked Ellie, sounding miffed that she hadn't been informed.

She bit her lip. "No, no. It's just that Jack—that is, Lord Leete —insisted on discussing something with me, and we lingered together long enough for the tabbies to notice."

"He *is* very handsome," murmured her maid. "And very amusing."

"He is also very annoying." She glanced at the ornate clock set over the main gallery. "And very late."

They completed yet another circuit, her impatience echoed in the *tap-tap* of her heels against the polished marble tiles.

"A lady usually only has that certain ruffled air about her when a gentleman is keeping her waiting." Angling out from the ornate Corinthian columns framing the Academy's entrance, Beaumont fell in step beside her. "Might I offer my company until the offending party arrives?"

Harriet decided there was no harm in engaging in a mild flirtation. Like most endeavors, it required practice to attain a modicum of skill. "You sound as if you speak from experience."

Beaumont's smile, she noted, had a vaguely feline quality to it. Perhaps because of his almond-shaped topaz eyes and fine-boned face, which tapered to a pointed chin. "It is permissible to be fashionably late," he answered.

"And pray tell, just how do you define fashionable?"

"Ah. An interesting question." He slowly stroked his chin.

Harriet wondered whether he had developed the habit to show off his beautifully manicured hands. His fingers were graceful, yet saved from being too feminine by a lean strength and hint of calluses around the tips. He was no pampered fop, despite the well-tended nails.

"Really, sir, don't tell me you haven't given it considerable thought. After all, you French have refined the concept of fashionable to a fine art."

He laughed softly. "You are interesting, Miss Farnum."

"You sound as if that surprises you," challenged Harriet.

"No, it intrigues me." Beaumont offered his arm. "Come walk with me. Whoever your friend is, he has now passed from being fashionably late to being unfashionably rude."

She accepted the offer, deciding it was too good an opportunity to learn more about the French émigré community in London. It did not seem Beaumont was on the best of terms with Amirault, and perhaps that could be turned to her advantage.

"Do you enjoy art, Monsieur?" she asked as they strolled into one of the exhibition rooms, Ellie trailing a few steps behind them.

"Yes, but not as much as other things."

Harriet made a point of taking her time to study a landscape painting by Constable before replying. "How provocative." Leaning closer to the canvas, she noted the subtle shading of color and texture of the brush strokes. A good reminder of how things could appear very different, depending on the point of view. "I assume you want me to ask what things, so I shall oblige you."

"I find human nature more compelling than painted scenes of storm-dark skies and distant hills, such as the one you are admiring," he answered.

"Art has layers of emotion that are nuanced and complex," pointed out Harriet.

"*Oui*, but they are never quite so viscerally alive in pigment and linseed oil as they are in flesh and blood, are they?"

"I'm not sure I entirely agree with you, sir."

Beaumont regarded her thoughtfully. "That is one of the beauties of art—it stirs so many personal reactions." He led her into one of the side salons. "If we are to admire art, I prefer portraits to outdoor scenes. It fascinates me to try to guess what the subjects are really thinking."

Harriet was careful to keep her expression neutral. Clearly he was trying to get under her skin with his sly probing, but for what reason? "The trouble is," she responded, "you see them through the artist's eyes, so you can't really count on getting a true picture."

"Truth." Beaumont flicked a mote of dust from his lapel. "You must be an extraordinary judge of character to think you may discern the truth about people simply by looking at their faces."

Her gaze remained locked on the Duchess of Devonshire's finely-wrought curls and impossibly rakish hat, as depicted by Gainsborough.

"Lovely, isn't she?" he commented, following her glance. "But as you pointed out, who would have guessed the duchess was a wild, reckless gambler by looking at that innocent expression."

"The hat gives her away," said Harriet without thinking. "It's outrageously daring. And the eyes. There's nothing innocent about her eyes."

He stepped forward and somehow his shoulder was now touching hers. The heat of him seemed to spear through the layers of wool and silk, sending a tiny frisson of awareness down her arm.

Beaumont must have felt her reaction for she saw his profile shift ever so slightly as the line of his mouth curled upward. The cat-clever gleam in his eye became more pronounced, sparking to a hue of sunburnt gold that matched the highlights of the duchess's tumbled tresses.

"I think that you are right. Those little things do give her away." His gaze now angled to her own features, its scrutiny moving over her skin like a physical caress.

Harriet repressed a shiver.

"I sense that very little escapes you, Miss Farnum. I shall have to be careful to keep my guard up."

"Have you something to hide?" she countered.

"Of course. Don't we all?"

Harriet moved on to the next painting.

"You are very good at it, you know." Some secret amusement shaded his voice. "But not quite good enough."

Her shoes scuffing on the smooth marble, she halted in confusion.

"Your expression," he said in a low voice. A step, swift and silent as a stalking panther, had brought him close enough that his breath stirred the tiny hairs on the back of her neck. "You hide your thoughts well, a skill I daresay you learned from being a diplomat's daughter. However, as you so sagely pointed out, the eyes can often betray us."

Unable to muster a clever retort, Harriet held her tongue. Uncertain of what she had given away, she turned back to the gilt-framed canvases on the wall. "So what dark longings do you see in this young man's eyes." She indicated a portrait of Gainsborough's nephew. "There's an obvious arrogance, but beneath that I see trepidation. What do you think he's afraid of?"

Beaumont refused to be diverted. "Take, for example, last night," he went on, as if he hadn't heard her. "Your tone is often tart with Lord Leete, and yet your gaze says that you care for him more than most people would guess."

"Of course I care for him," replied Harriet calmly, though she was furiously wracking her brain, trying to recall having seen the Frenchman anywhere in the ballroom. But all she saw were spinning shadows and hazed faces. Her attention had all been on Jack. "Leete is a good friend of my older brother. We have known each other for years."

Beaumont's voice dropped a notch. "Then I would guess you do not wish to see him come to grief. He's suffered enough from French steel, eh?"

A chill gripped her, as if a blade of ice had skated down her spine.

"W-What do you mean?" she asked, hoping the tremor was too slight to resonate in her throat.

As he shifted his weight, a curl came to the corners of his mouth, and in that slight gesture she knew he was not fooled in the least. He knew he had frightened her.

"Only that questions tend to upset a certain group of my countrymen residing here in England."

"Including you?"

In answer, he gave a Gallic shrug. "You may wish to pass on the information to His Lordship."

"What information?" The Frenchman wasn't the only man who could move on cat's paws when he so chose.

Jack's stealthy approach startled Harriet, but Beaumont

appeared unperturbed. "That you are unconscionably late, Monsieur. A gentleman ought never keep a lady waiting." Relinquishing his spot beside her with a courtly bow, he backed off. "Keep a close eye on the faces around you, Miss Farnum," he added in a low whisper, just loud enough for her to hear, "And be watchful."

With that, he bowed again and strolled through the archway of the adjoining salon.

"What was that all about?" demanded Jack.

Frowning, Harriet watched the flutter of his coat tails disappear behind the fluted columns framing the opening, uncomfortably aware that whatever game had just been played, she had been beaten badly.

"I wish I knew."

CHAPTER 13

Jack watched her face, reminded yet again that of late he was having a hard time reading the play of emotions. His own feelings were equally confusing. Exasperation over her stubborn insistence on charging into danger tangled with the realization that he had come to depend on her common sense and camaraderie. And more troubling was the thread of worry that he had drawn her into a nest of vipers.

"Harry, I don't want you dealing with these Frenchmen," he growled. "Your help with deciphering the secrets held in the papers is more than enough."

In a very un-Harriet reaction, she merely shifted her gaze to the paintings on the wall. Silence loomed between them, with a weight that seemed to press against his chest.

"Harry…"

"What do you see when you look at this face?" she asked abruptly, a slight nod indicating a large portrait from the previous century framed in age-dark oak.

"A fellow who looks like he's cursed bored with having to sit still for the artist," he grumbled.

"Be serious." Her eyes remained on the painting. "Didn't you ever look—really look—at the paintings of your ancestors that hang along the main stairway at Hendrie Hall and try to discern what they were like as individuals?"

"No, my attention was more focused on wishing I had the fourth Earl's nose rather than that of my mother's grandfather," he shot back.

Harriet huffed a sigh.

Jack took a grudging step closer to the painting and studied the face. "Sorry, but I am a simple fellow. I see a slightly arrogant fop, whose shirt frills look deucedly uncomfortable. Beyond that, I don't discern the nuances that you seem to expect of me."

The answer deepened the furrow between her brows.

He tried to ignore it, but the sense that he had somehow disappointed her made him look again. For all his posturing, Gainsborough was actually an artist he admired. There was, he admitted, a depth to the man's art. An ability to probe beneath the skin-deep smiles.

It made him think more carefully about Harriet's question. His experience in military intelligence during his day on the Peninsula had taught him to pay close attention to expressions and gesture. One could tell much about a man by watching him interact with his friends. And his enemies.

"Very well, since it seems so deucedly important to you, I'll play along with your game." Jack squinted, making a show of studious examination. "The fellow's gaze is oblique, he's not willing to meet the world head-on."

Harriet nodded. "And why is that, I wonder? To me, he has a slyness about him. I wouldn't trust him."

"I don't deny that one can read much in a man's face—"

"Or a lady's," she murmured.

"Be that as it may, it is just one way of judging character," he went on. "Some people see details better than others." His words triggered an odd sensation, and for an instant he hesitated, trying to give substance to the shadowy image that was suddenly hovering at the edge of his consciousness.

"What is it?" she asked.

Jack closed his eyes for an instant, willing himself to bring it into focus. *A face?* It swirled, maddeningly elusive, and then dipped and darted back into the darkness. "Nothing. Your comments about studying the painted faces brought something to mind, but it's gone now."

"I find it interesting to observe people," she mused.

Several of Harriet's pithy comments about the school friends her brother had brought home from Eton and Oxford rose up from his memory. "I'm not quite sure how you do it, but whether it is by sorcery or witchcraft, you are skilled at discerning a person's strengths." His mouth gave an involuntary quirk. "And weaknesses."

"Am I?"

Jack was unused to hearing her words resonate with such uncertainty. Which made him suspect she was holding something back.

Taking her arm, he drew her out into the corridor and found a spot by one of the mullioned windows. The light, freshly scrubbed by a passing rain shower, helped to cleanse the shadows from her features. "What did that damnable Frog do to upset you?"

Harriet looked down at the marble floor tiles, as if some answer might be hidden among the subtle veins of color running through the stone.

"Harry?"

A grimace pulled at her lips. "He made me realize I'm not nearly as good at it as I thought I was."

"Explain yourself," he demanded tersely.

She looked for a moment as if to fight him. *Cross swords. En garde. Thrust and parry.* Most of the time he enjoyed the duels. But not now. Not with that inscrutable look lurking beneath her lashes. "And be advised that I shall be relentless until I have the answer out of you. My steel is sharper than yours."

She flinched at the word "steel." Feeling like a brute, he touched her arm and smiled. "Metaphorically speaking, that is."

Her features slowly relaxed into an answering grin. "I am impressed. I thought you were booted out of Oxford before you learned any big words."

"I learned them from you, who are far wiser than any of the prosy professors who tried to whack some knowledge through my thick skull with their boring lectures."

Harriet was never boring, Infuriating at times, but never boring.

"At least you are smart enough to realize that." The momentary note of whimsy faded. "But as I said, wisdom did me little good against Mr. Beaumont's crafty cleverness. He maneuvered me into thinking I was parrying his probing on one front, then all of a sudden he skillfully slipped a blade in under my guard before retreating without a scratch." Her hands knotted together. "I feel like the veriest of fools."

Jack twined his fingers around hers and drew them apart. They were chilled, and without thinking, he gently chafed them between his palms. "You aren't making any sense yet."

"Yes, I know. I'm still aghast at my hubris." Harriet didn't try to pull away. "Thinking myself skilled at the art of subtle interrogation, I thought perhaps I could coax some useful information out of Beaufort. I was impressed with how well I matched his air of jaded cynicism."

Jack was already itching to take the man's fancy cravat and knot it tighter around his throat.

"And I was busy framing my first cunning question, when all of a sudden, he surprised me." She took a moment to compose her thoughts. "Nay, shocked me is a more honest description."

Despite his own impatience, he waited in silence, allowing her to get to the heart of what was upsetting her at her own pace.

It came out in a rush. "Beaumont knew about the attack on you."

"Is *that* what has you in such a pucker?" Jack refrained from adding a chuckle. "It's likely common knowledge within the émigré community. People find it hard to keep secrets. They talk among their friends. It is a universal weakness of human nature."

"Yes..." She didn't say it aloud, and yet the word *but* crackled in the air.

"But what?" he growled.

"He implied that if you keep asking questions, it could be very dangerous."

At that, Jack did let out a gruff laugh. "Harry, I am no stranger to danger. Over the past few years, we have developed a comfortable camaraderie, but on the battlefield, I've proved I'm not such a frivolous fellow." A spasm of emotion rippled through her eyes, its intensity catching him by surprise. "I was caught off-guard once," he added softly. "It won't happen again."

"How can you be so sure?" she shot back. "I—I am worried about you. Perhaps it would be best to back away from this. Not every conundrum needs to be solved."

"That's unlike you. When you get a bone between your teeth, you are usually fiercer than a bull mastiff in keeping hold of it," he drawled to cover the odd little lurch he felt inside his chest.

"It's no jesting matter, you big lummox!" snapped Harriet. "Though why I should care about your hide if you don't is beyond me."

Their eyes locked for an instant, and the blaze of fury nearly singed his lashes. Then she broke away with a low huff and signaled to her maid, who was standing a discreet distance away between a pair of ancient Greek statues.

"Come along, Ellie," she said in a tightly coiled voice. "I think I have seen enough art for the day."

Jack watched her march off, skirts frothing like storm-churned waves around her ankles. Bemusement warred with a far more complex swirl of feelings, ones he didn't quite care to examine at the moment.

Instead, he headed back to the portrait gallery, hoping another turn through the paintings might help recall the fleeting image that had flashed through his thoughts. He couldn't shake the feeling that it was somehow important.

Faces, faces. He paused in front of the oak-framed gentleman who had caught Harriet's attention. The eyes. She had focused on the eyes.

He tried to recall from his brief Oxford studies who had said that the eyes were the windows to the soul? Was it Shakespeare? Milton? Plato? As he stood trying to puzzle it out, the image flitted back into his head. It was clearer this time, sharpening to a pair of smoke-tinged orbs. *Closer, closer.* Something about the nose was taking shape, but still, the whole face remained elusive.

Lost in thought, Jack turned away from the paintings and headed for the exit.

HARRIET WAS STILL SEETHING the next day, and sorely tempted to fling all her copious notes on Madame La Rochelle's missing husband into the fire. The coals crackled, echoing the sound of the papers as she swept them up from her desk.

It would serve Jack right for being such a mule-headed sapskull.

But at the last moment, something held her back. "I suppose I'm just as mule-headed as he is," she muttered under her breath. Jack would, she knew, ignore the warnings and be careless about his safety. So it was up to her to unravel the mystery. Beaumont's words of caution had not been aimed at her, that much she was sure. So far, no one save Jack knew of her involvement, and she meant to keep it that way.

But it would demand more expertise than she had shown yesterday.

The fancy clothes and new-found grace had made her over-confident, a foolish mistake she would not make again. Whatever plot was afoot, the conspirators would be far more experienced in deception and manipulation than she was. There could be no more mistakes.

"But I have shown that I can polish new skills in a hurry if I put my mind to it," she told herself, setting down the pile of notes next to her open journal. A glance at the page reminded her the weekly meeting at Lady Catherine's townhouse was scheduled to begin shortly.

And if she didn't begin dressing for the occasion, she was going to be late. It was a pity that Theo would not be there to help give the account of the ball. But her mother had demanded her presence at tea for an old friend, and a sense of duty had caused her friend to cry off from the current meeting. As for future ones...

Harriet shook off her disappointment. As she well knew, it wasn't easy to know which battles to fight and which were better served by a strategic retreat.

An hour later, attired in one of her stylish new walking gowns —as promised to the others, who wanted to see Mrs. McNulty's artistry in the flesh—Harriet was just passing into the entrance foyer of Lady Catherine's townhouse when the clatter of hurried steps sounded behind her.

"Wait," called a breathless Theo to the butler as he made to shut the door.

"I thought you weren't coming," murmured Harriet.

"I decided that I really wished to attend these meetings. I enjoy the new ideas, and the new friends I have made," answered Theo, as she untied the string of her chipstraw bonnet. "And so I told my mother so."

"Oh, dear."

"Well, not in quite so many words." Theo's mouth curled up. "I simply told her it was a group of very interesting ladies, and that they were the ones who arranged my entrée onto Madame Deauville's client list."

"Very clever," said Harriet.

"I am learning."

"I wish I could say the same for myself." Then, ruing her words, she quickly took her friend's arm. "We had better go in. I'm sure everyone is impatient to start the agenda, so there will be plenty of time at tea for hearing about our Grand Adventure."

Theo, however, dug in her heels. "You sound overset. What's wrong?"

Harriet didn't wish to lie. "I'm just a little preoccupied, is all."

"I had wondered whether you and Jack were having a disagreement the other night," ventured her friend.

"That is nothing new. Jack and I are *always* disagreeing about something," she replied dryly. "He was being particularly stubborn on a certain matter, but I shall deal with it."

"If you need—"

"Gels, gels—come take a seat!" clucked Miss Breville as she crossed from one of the side parlors with a book in hand and made shooing motions toward the drawing room. "We have much to discuss on John Locke's philosophy today." Her solemn expression was lightened by a slight twinkle from behind the lenses of her spectacles. "And perhaps a less cerebral topic, assuming we have time."

Not unhappy to escape further probing from her friend, Harriet dutifully led the way to the circle of chairs.

The discussion proved more lively than usual. Words and ideas spun round and round, like so many glittering couples twirling together across a dance floor.

"It seems," remarked Mrs. Currough during a brief lull in the talk, "that we are all anxious to race through our intellectual gavotte and turn to the fairytale elegance of the waltz."

Guilty chuckles greeted the observation. "Well, since you mention it, I have worked up quite an appetite for tea and cakes," said Miss Ashmun.

"And sugar-spun romance," teased Mrs. Griffin, who did not look to have a romantic bone in her body.

But as Harriet well knew, appearances could be deceiving.

"However frivolous it may be," went one Mrs. Griffin, "I confess that I am all atwitter to hear an account of the storybook evening our friends just attended."

With that, the group quickly agreed to defer further debate on Locke to the following week. "There is nothing wrong with a little frivolity. Life is all about striking a balance," said Lady Catherine as she rang for refreshments. "Laughter and gaiety are just as important as serious thought on abstract ideals."

An expectant hush filled the room as soon as the clink of cups and plates had settled down. It was Mrs. McNulty who, after dusting the sugary crumbs from her fingertips, took charge of the proceedings.

"I do wish you all could have seen the ballgowns," she began. "Harriet and Theo looked absolutely magnificent at the final fitting. The watered silk we chose for them, a special weave from the south of India, draped like a dream..." The dressmaker went on to describe in great detail the cut and the trimmings, ending with a soulful sigh.

"I do wish that someday I could experience the splendor of a Mayfair mansion ballroom," she added after a sip of her now-tepid tea. "Sparkling champagne, polished marble and gilded moldings, fluted columns and pedestals festooned with fancy flowers, music floating through the perfume-scented air..." Her eyes closed for a moment, and a dreamy smile flitted soft as moonlight over her lips. "What a treat it would be to see my creations spinning and shimmering in the cut-crystal candlelight."

Harriet was ashamed to realize that she hadn't thought about that. The ladies of the *ton* might beg for the services of Madame Deauville, but no matter the effusive compliments and the generous gifts that showered upon her, never would a woman in trade be invited to one of their fancy parties. Basking in the glow of her marvelous labor could happen only in the realm of imagination.

That, vowed Harriet, would soon change...

"Oh, do describe every glorious detail for us," urged Miss Ashmun, interrupting her thoughts with a plea and a beseeching glance.

Suddenly feeling even more unsettled, Harriet looked to Theo. "Why don't you begin. I feel in need of another cup of tea."

After hesitating a fraction, her gaze clouding in question, Theo began to describe the glittering scene. Her voice was hesitant at first, then took on greater confidence as her shyness gave way to the fun of recreating the swirling splendor of the ball. The glittering ladies swathed in their jeweltone colors and shiny baubles, the elegant gentlemen in their tailored finery, the lilting notes of the music...

Harriet quietly rose and moved to the tea table by the bowfront window. Turning her back to the group, she set her cup down and stared through the rain-spattered glass at the mist skirling through the square. Perhaps it was Jack's comment about vipers, but the vaporous tendrils suddenly took on the look of writhing snakes, slithering over the wet cobbles.

Caught up in her own brooding, it took her a moment to notice she wasn't alone.

"Your tea is cold," murmured Mrs. Currough. "Shall I ring for a fresh pot?"

Harriet shook her head. "I just needed a breath of air to clear my thoughts."

"The air," said the Irish Beauty, "does not appear to have blown away the storm clouds."

A rueful huff leached from her lungs, but she tried to make

light of her brooding. "True, and the weather looks to be getting worse."

"Any particular reason?"

How to answer? A coil of conflicting feelings seemed to have tangled inside her head, their smoke-dark shadows hazing her brain. But if there was anyone who could offer advice, it was the worldly courtesan.

"I think that in following your advice, I assumed a false sense of invincibility along with my straighter spine, and regal hauteur," she finally whispered. "You explained that dress and deportment are all about illusion. And yet I told myself I was oh-so wise and clever, and actually believed it because I wanted to think it true."

"Wisdom is a devilishly difficult thing to acquire," replied Mrs. Currough. "And to judge. I daresay you are less foolish than you think you are at this moment."

"Would that were true." Harriet picked up a biscuit and then merely crumbled it between her fingers. "Y-You are an expert on men. Am I a peagoose to think I can match wits with them?"

The Irish Beauty's gaze followed hers out to the broad swath of garden and surrounding cobbled streets. The rain was coming down in great sheets of wind-whipped water. "Now that is a question for which there is no easy answer."

From behind them sounded a peal of laughter. Theo was describing one of the foppish young men who fancied himself among the leading arbiters of style. He had appeared at the ball wearing starched shirt points that threatened to gouge out his eyes and a turquoise wasp-waisted coat with brass buttons the size of tea saucers.

Harriet felt equally absurd.

But to her surprise, Mrs. Currough continued, once the giggles died down. "I am quite certain that women are equal to men in intelligence. It's a matter of how you use your strength." Looking thoughtful, she gathered her skirts and perched a hip on the edge of the table. "Think of it this way—most men aren't equally matched in physical strength. If it comes down to fisticuffs, some may try to use brute force to win, while others will have to depend on guile or speed. It's a matter of knowing your own strengths and your opponent's weaknesses."

"Thank you," she said with a tentative smile. "That's exceedingly helpful."

"I am always happy to answer questions. Not that I always have the answers."

"Even with your experience?"

An unreadable look dances beneath the Mrs. Currough's gold-tipped lashes. "Yes, even with my experience, I too, can feel the fool."

Harriet was about to turn back to the group when she ventured a parting query. "Just one last thing. Do men ever get any less infuriating?"

The Irish Beauty's lips quivered in silent mirth. "Never. But that is their charm. We would likely grow bored with them if they ever stopped setting off sparks."

"Ha! There are times when I am heartily sick of getting scorch marks on my skin."

Mrs. Currough slowly traced a fingertip down one of the fogged windowpanes, leaving a dark line in the silver-gray condensation. "Ice is far worse." Seeing Lady Catherine cast an inquiring look their way, she gave a small nod. "Now, we had best rejoin our friends."

Theo looked around as Harriet slid into her seat. "I've done my best, but you have a more discerning eye and are better at painting a scene. I shall gladly allow you to continue."

Happy to see her friend losing her shyness with strangers, Harriet demurred. "I have been listening, and you've done a splendid job."

"Aye, I can almost hear the violins and pianoforte echoing off the crystal chandeliers," said Mrs. Griffin with a gusty sigh. "I do so love Mozart."

"So I've really nothing to add."

Lady Catherine, who occasionally enjoyed provoking a bit of controversy, fixed Harriet with a sidelong look, and then murmured, "Theo neglected to mention your dance partners. Was your handsome gentleman friend—that tall, broad-shouldered, dark-as-the-devil fellow—present, and did he ask you to waltz?"

Harriet colored as a titter of *oohs* and *aahs* traveled around the circle.

"This gets better and better!" exclaimed Miss Ashmun. "*What gentleman?*"

Lady Catherine was discreet enough not to mention the dramatic circumstances involved in meeting Jack, but she did raise a teasing brow in support of the question. "Yes, do tell. The papers mentioned Lord 'L' was in your presence for much of the evening."

"He is an old family friend," stammered Harriet.

Theo nodded in support. "Yes, a friend. From her brother's school days."

"Who has seen the gosling transform into a swan," murmured Lady Catherine.

Sensing Harriet's discomfort, Theo quickly changed the subject. "Oh, I almost forgot to tell you all about the supper room, where the tables were laden with all sorts of sumptuous delicacies..." A lengthy recitation followed.

"Lobster patties with cream sauce," repeated Miss Breville faintly. "Good Heavens, that sounds very decadent—but divine."

The others looked a trifle disappointed that the talk of men had given way to shellfish and butter, but the remaining quarter hour of the meeting passed cheerfully in a debate over which flavor of the special sorbets sounded the most exotic.

Feeling a rush of relief when the tall case clock in the corridor signaled the end of the gathering, Harriet shot up from her chair and took a hasty leave. That Theo had her own carriage waiting was also welcome. She longed for silence during the ride home, and Ellie could be counted on to gauge her current mood and remain silent.

Lady Currough's words had given her much to mull over.

Strengths and weaknesses. Would that she could be a dispassionate judge of her own heart.

CHAPTER 14

*J*ack turned up the collar of his coat to ward off the damp chill seeping into the darkened carriage. "Hell's bells," he grumbled, twitching back the window draperies for another quick glance up and down the side street. "How can ladies talk this long about political philosophy?"

The only answer was the rattle of glass as the rising breeze gusted against the windowpanes.

Uttering a low oath, he slouched back and crossed his arms.

After waiting for what felt like an age, the squish of steps through the puddles finally sounded.

Setting his hand on the inside latch, he waited until Harriet had mounted the iron rungs and cracked open the door before pulling it open and yanking her inside.

"Quiet," he hissed, clamping a hand over her mouth and rapping on the trap with the other. The coachman flicked his whip and the horses set off.

"What the devil are you doing here?" she snapped, as soon as he released her. "And where is Ellie?"

"At Gunter's," he replied, rubbing his sore shoulder. "Damn Wills for teaching you to throw such a hard punch."

"He wanted me to know how to defend myself against brutes," Harriet retorted with a hint of satisfaction.

"Well, next time you feel the urge to practice as a pugilist, hit someone else," groused Jack.

She settled herself against the squabs. "I ask again, what are you doing here?"

"Hoping to have a private conversation." Reaching up, he struck a flint to steel and lit the oil lamp. The flame wavered, then brightened, painting her scowl in an oily light. "Sorry, it's rather important, so I didn't wish to wait."

At that, Harriet sat up a little straighter. "What's happened?"

"Your talk about faces at the Royal Academy yesterday stirred up a memory from the afternoon I was attacked. It was only a fleeting glance, and it was jumbled in the rush of all the other things until you reminded me of it. But a shaft of light broke through the clouds just as I spun around, and in that moment I saw there was a man lurking in the side alleyway, watching what was happening."

"Red Lion Square is not far from the rookeries, Jack," she pointed out. "Men looking for trouble sometimes stray into the area."

"This was no ordinary footpad or cracksman," he replied.

A frown pinched between her brows. "Are you saying you recognized him?"

Jack nodded. "Yes. It was Pierre La Rochelle's batman."

"Are you sure?" she asked slowly. "As you said, the glimpse was only for an instant and you were under duress."

"I am quite sure," he replied. "Etienne Verdunne has a very distinctive broken nose. I saw it countless times during my recovery, as he helped tend to me during the French army's retreat. It is indelibly imprinted in my mind's eye."

"Ye God," muttered Harriet. "That would mean..." Her gaze slid down to her lap, leaving the rest of the thought unspoken.

"That would mean that after saving me from the grave, my dear friends apparently now want me dead."

Her hands twined together in a tight knot. "There may be some other explanation."

A laugh, bitter-tasting as bile, rose up in his throat. "I am willing to hear it."

When she didn't answer, Jack stretched out his legs, trying to uncoil the twist of pain in his gut. Confiding in Harriet had somehow eased the hurt a little, though it did nothing to salve the sense of utter betrayal.

"How could I have misjudged Camille so badly?" he uttered softly.

"Because you are the soul of honor and can't imagine such a treacherous lack of loyalty," answered Harriet stoutly.

His lips compressed in a thin smile. "You make me sound like a naïve schoolboy."

"No, I make you sound like a man of integrity."

The jangling of the harness sounded loud as gunfire in the moment of silence that followed.

"Thank you for that, Harry," he whispered. "It makes me feel less like a bloody fool."

Harriet found his hand and carefully unclenched his fisted fingers. "You may be a stubborn arse at times," she murmured. "But never a fool."

The carriage wheels bumped and jolted over the uneven pavement, and yet Jack felt his muscles relax. Her friendship was a balm for bruised spirits.

"Assuming you are not mistaken about the man you saw, the question is why are you enough of a threat to them that they want you dead?"

"You can be assured I have been asking myself the same question, and so far, I can't come up with an answer."

"Well, then, let us think harder." Her chin took on a determined tilt, a look that did not bode well for any conundrum that dared stand in her way. "We must apply logic. You have either seen or heard something that endangers them, or they fear you are close to uncovering a vital clue. And since you've been trying to trace the whereabouts of Pierre La Rochelle, it seems likely it has to do with him."

Jack nodded.

"Perhaps his batman had been bribed to help one of the émigré factions kill him, and they are afraid you will uncover the truth."

"Have you considered writing horrid novels?" asked Jack drily. "You have a very vivid imagination."

"You have to admit, it's plausible."

He scrubbed a hand over his jaw. "I suppose so." And yet, his mind rebelled against believing it. Etienne had been a very pleasant fellow, and seemingly devoted to Pierre. But with the wavering lamplight weaving in and out of the darkness, and the rain drumming down on the varnished wood of the carriage, he was aware of how easily perceptions could become twisted.

Harriet was watching his face carefully. "There's another possibility. You will like it even less."

As he shifted, his dark hair fell across his face, curtaining his expression.

"Go on."

"You won't like," Harriet said again in warning, trying to gauge his reaction.

The shadows gave nothing away.

"You have said before that you can't believe that Camille would be involved in any attempt on your life," she said, trying to keep her voice flat and devoid of emotion. "You're convinced that she is desperate to find her husband, and any erratic behavior is spurred by confusion and fear, rather than any less laudable emotions. But have you considered that she is not being forthright with you? Perhaps she isn't as anxious as you believe to be reunited."

"And yet she is here in England," replied Jack. "How does your logic explain that?"

"In any number of ways." Was it only jealousy that had her so easily imagining the range of possibilities?

The whisper of wool brushed over the leather seat as he crossed his legs. "Such as?"

"Perhaps she and the batman are amorously involved, and they have come to England in order to do away with the inconvenient spouse." The image of Amirault's handsome face flitted through her mind's eye. "Or perhaps she's secretly a Royalist and has been involved with the Comte for some time. It seems a rather odd coincidence that she has turned to him for advice. Or... I could go on and on. There are a great many more speculations I could make."

"Each more lurid than the last," he growled.

"Someone tried to murder you, Jack."

His silence was unreadable.

Leaning back, Harriet said nothing more. The air in the carriage, heavy with vapor and smoke, was oppressive. Her damp skirts were tangled uncomfortably around her legs.

"So what would you suggest I do?" he asked abruptly. "Heed Beaumont's warning and back away from further questions in hopes that they won't come after me again?"

"And if I said yes, would you heed *me*?"

A flicker of light danced down the curl of his smile. "That would be the reasonable thing to do, but as you pointed out, I'm a stubborn arse. Now that I've been drawn into this devil-cursed mystery, I mean to learn the truth of what is going on, no matter where it leads."

Her gaze roamed over the tiny cracks and crevasses etched into the age-dark wood paneling. "Then we need to map out a strategy. Right now it seems obvious that Camille, Amirault, Beaumont and Etienne Verdun are somehow intertwined—and at the heart of the spiderweb of questions is the missing Pierre La Rochelle. But the answers won't be easy to unravel."

"It's done one thread at a time," said Jack. "I've several old military comrades I can call on for a favor. One can tell me more about the émigré factions and their activities, and one has the resources to delve into the underworld and track Etienne Verdun to ground."

That leaves Camille, thought Harriet, feeling a lurch in her stomach that had nothing to do with the carriage wheels rolling over the uneven stones. Steadying herself on the seat, she repeated the thought aloud.

"Yes, Camille," mused Jack, sinking deeper into a slouch. His lashes lowered, enough that she was sure his eyes had fallen shut.

Loath to interrupt his reveries, Harriet toyed with the cuff of her new gown, studying the intricate stitching and delicate lace. A great deal of meticulous work, she noted, went into fashioning such a small detail.

"I have been thinking," he finally announced.

"I thought perhaps you had been sleeping."

His brows flicked up in mock outrage. "I can, on occasion, use my brain," he drawled. "Which I shall endeavor to prove. Hear me out. I trust you will think me exceedingly clever."

"I am waiting," she said, "with bated breath."

"During one of my first meetings with Camille—that day, in fact, when I first encountered you in Red Lion Square—she inquired about my friendship with you, and asked about arranging for her to meet your father."

Harriet looked up in surprise. "You never mentioned that."

"Because I immediately told her that I wouldn't consider such a thing. It was clear that she hoped to coax a favor from him with her womanly wiles, and it struck me as a shabby thing to do to both you and Pierre."

"That explains her interest in me," she mused. "At the ball, she seemed anxious to form a friendship with me. She was pressing to meet for tea at Gunter's, and was the one who suggested a visit to the Royal Academy—though Beaufort interrupted that plan."

With this new information, her earlier wild speculations, said half in jest, no longer seemed so far-fetched. "I assumed it was to learn more about you and your life in England. However, this gives a new perspective to things. The interest in my father is puzzling. What did she hope to gain?"

"Influence, information, access to people who could help find answers quickly. A senior diplomat who wields power within the government could be very useful in finding Pierre."

"Assuming she is looking for him," responded Harriet.

He expelled a long sigh. "Yes, but—"

"Amirault also evinced interest in my father when he struck up a flirtation with me last week." Suddenly recalling the interlude, Harriet couldn't refrain from overriding his words. "That cannot have been coincidence," she said, a sense of rising excitement taking hold of her. "I need to draw out the reason."

Jack let out a loud growl.

"Let me finish," she chided. "Then you can snap and snarl."

He glowered but kept his jaw clenched. She could swear she heard his molars grinding over the carriage sounds.

"I'll need a bold approach, an unexpected angle. They are both clever and won't give themselves away easily. But my advantage is they underestimate me. Amirault sees a wren who is suddenly wearing peacock's plumage, so likely he thinks me a desperate young lady who is thinking of naught but attracting a husband."

Another sound reverberated in his throat.

"And Camille views me in much the same way," she hurried on, before it could explode into words. "A rather dim-witted unsophisticated English lady who isn't capable of matching wits with a worldly French woman of the world. I shall find a way to use their assumptions against them."

"Are you done?" Jack asked politely, though an ominous undertone shaded his voice. "Am I now finally permitted to speak?"

Harriet nodded.

"Good. Perhaps now I may finish my own thoughts."

She folded her hands in her lap.

"Which were much the same as yours in terms of drawing them out. But we will do so together."

"Jack, that is not practical. People are already beginning to titter. If we are to be seen spending a great deal of time together, it will provoke gossip." A clattering of the carriage forced her to pause for a moment. "Not to speak of reflect badly on your reputation."

"*My* reputation?" he asked in an odd voice.

"Yes, as a dashing, devil-may-care rogue with a dark and dangerous reputation with the ladies." Her mouth quirked. "Dancing attendance on me will dull your horns and pitchfork."

"You did suggest a bold strategy, both imaginative and unexpected."

Harriet eyed him warily, trying to spot whatever verbal trap he seemed to be setting.

"Well, I have thought of something very clever that will kill two birds with one stone."

He so looked vastly pleased with himself that she felt compelled to say, "Pray, don't keep me in suspense."

Jack turned his big body, and suddenly the seat felt very small. His leg was half-lost in the folds of her skirts, and the closeness was sending strange pulses of heat up and down the length of her limbs.

"It's really quite simple. We shall announce our engagement."

Harriet nearly slid off the soft leather and landed on his knee. "Are you mad?" she demanded, once she had regained control of her vocal cords. "You can't ask me to marry you?"

"Why not?"

Because you don't love me, you infuriating man! she wanted to shout.

"To begin with, because you don't want to be married."

"I said we shall announce our engagement," pointed out Jack. "I did not say we would actually go through with the ceremony. That is the clever part."

Harriet blinked, angry to feel the prickle of tears against the inside of her eyelids.

"Ladies are allowed to cry off without consequence, so you may end it and no one will think badly of you." A rueful smile tugged up one side of his mouth, giving him a boyish lopsided smile that made her heart hit up against her ribcage. "Indeed, no one will blame you in the least for cutting line with such a ramshackle fellow as me."

Harriet couldn't bear to look at him any longer.

"So you may walk away when we have finished our investigation. But in the meantime, it affords us the perfect reason for being in each other's pockets. And it may prove useful in creating some interesting interplay between us and Camille and Amirault. If they have plans of using you, my presence may make them have to improvise, and in my experience, that is when people can make mistakes."

She kept her gaze focused on the sliver of windowglass showing through the gap in the draperies, thankful that the familiar landmarks of Mayfair were finally rolling into sight.

"Yet another thing," Jack added, "is you will be doing me a great favor by saving me from all the managing Mamas who are anxious to dangle their eligible daughters under my nose. I feel like a fox being pursued by a rapacious pack of hounds."

"Ah, well, if I can be *useful*, then I shall of course seriously consider it," replied Harriet a little acidly.

Jack finally seemed to sense her mood. He leaned in closer, the masculine scent of bay rum and smoke teasing and tickling at her nostrils. "Are you upset about something?"

She inched away only to find her shoulder pressed up against the paneling. "I am troubled about a number of things," she muttered, not wanting to give herself away.

"Harry..." He set his hand on her forearm, a casual touch and yet she nearly came undone. "Damnation, I'm sorry to have drawn you into this muddle. You've every right to be angry with me. You ought to be dancing until dawn with the bevy of admirers clinging to your skirts, not studying reams of papers, or consorting with duplicitous Frenchmen on my behalf."

"I don't dance particularly well," said Harriet. "And the only admirers clinging to my skirts are pompous popinjays. Solving problems is far more interesting."

Jack raised a brow. "Then what is your objection to my suggestion? It seems an eminently practical way of attacking the conundrum."

Practical. Harriet was beginning to loathe the word. However, he was right that the idea held some intriguing advantages. And the chance to best the supremely confident Camille La Rochelle at her own game was awfully alluring.

"It would serve you right if I said yes," she muttered under her breath.

"Yes? Was that a yes?" His face wreathed in a broad smile. "Excellent!" He caught her in a hard hug, squeezing the breath from her lungs. "We make a good team, Harry. You won't regret it."

CHAPTER 15

"Congratulations!" called one of the wags as Jack made his way through the reading room of White's. "Or should I say, commiserations! I hadn't realized you were badly dipped in the pocket."

Jack paused in mid-stride. "What makes you think that, Jenkins?"

"A plump dowry, ha, ha, ha." The baronet chuckled at his own wit. "It's said Miss Farnum is worth ten thousand a year."

With whisper-soft steps over the Oriental carpet, Jack approached the leather armchair. "Are you implying that I asked for the lady's hand merely for money?"

"Er, well, why else would a blade of your repute leave off cutting a swath through the boudoirs?"

"I am not at all interested in your speculations about my personal motives. What I do care about is that you keep a respectful tongue concerning my betrothed." Jack reached down and grasped the baronet's cravat, deliberately crushing the starched folds. "Else next time you shall find it yanked out and fed to the Tower ravens."

"N-No offense intended, Leete. Just a friendly jest, is all."

"Miss Farnum is not a jesting matter. Do I make myself clear?"

"Q-Quite."

Heads ducked in a flurry of rustling newspapers as Jack released his hold and looked around with a scowl. Hearing no further comments, he continued on into one of the private meeting rooms and quickly poured himself a brandy.

"Are you considering a career on the stage?" asked James, as he entered the room a moment later. "That was quite a magnificent performance."

"Stubble the sarcasm," he snapped. "I'm in no mood for it." He raised his glass, then set it aside untouched. "This betrothal business is harder work than I imagined."

His cousin Hermione had insisted on hosting a fancy supper party in honor of the announcement, while his father and the Duke of Pierpont were conspiring to throw another gala ball, this one in London, to celebrate the impending nuptials. Even Harriet's father, who was known for his stone-faced reserve, had allowed an expression of moderate pleasure on hearing the news. Jack couldn't help feeling a stab of guilt on thinking how disappointed they all would be when it ended.

As for Harriet...

"At least you don't have to go through the interminable rounds of morning calls that ladies must endure. Every matron in Mayfair is clamoring for a visit from Harriet," said James as he walked to the window and looked down on St. James's Street. "Theo tells me the two of them have drunk enough tea over the last few days to float the Channel Fleet."

"Thank God for Theo's staunch support," replied Jack. "Harriet does not enjoy the rituals of the *ton*." Another frisson of guilt stirred in the pit of his stomach. "She would be lost having to go through them on her own."

"They are fast friends. And friends stand by each other." James turned and perched a hip on the windowsill. "Which I suppose explains why I am here at this cursedly early hour with you, instead of sleeping comfortably in my bed."

"My apologies if I dragged you from the arms of the luscious Lucinda."

A clouded expression flitted over his friend's face. "Actually we parted ways a fortnight ago. Quite amicably, I might add, a sentiment encouraged by a hideously expensive bauble from Rundell & Bridge."

"Have you another ladybird in mind?" asked Jack.

"I thought I was summoned from my sleep to discuss *your* affairs, not mine."

"You aren't usually so irascible in the morning," observed Jack, after deciding to quaff a swallow of his brandy after all.

"Pour me a glass. It's bad luck to drink alone," said James morosely. "And then kindly tell me why I am here."

"I need to ask another favor concerning the French émigré community. But you'll have to be very careful—there could be some danger involved."

His friend's expression perked up.

"I had better explain, though it goes without saying that it must remain confidential." Though Jack summed up the conundrum as simply as he could, it took some minutes to explain the gist of it.

"A missing officer, a suspicious wife, who is somehow entangled in the warring faction of the French Royalists," mused James. "I think, perhaps, I need a hearty breakfast in order to chew over all this."

"You shall have it. But first, are you still friends with your old valet and his circle of friends?" James's former servant had decided that arranging business dealings in the underworld was a more lucrative profession than serving as a gentleman's gentleman.

"Yes, Rafferty has on occasion proved useful to know, so I maintain cordial relations with him. What is it you need?"

"I want him to find a Frenchman named Etienne Verdunne. My guess is the fellow is recently arrived in London," answered Jack. "And to detain him for questioning. I shall, of course, make it worth his while."

"I'll arrange it," assured James.

"Do so discreetly. Verdunne was involved in trying to put a period to my existence. As I said, I don't want to draw you into danger."

His friend let out a rude sound. "Danger may be just what I need to slay the blue devils that seem to have taken up residence in my head." As he pushed away from the window, a new alertness seemed to have displaced his earlier lethargy. "I have a good idea of where to find Raff at this hour."

"What about breakfast?"

"Lend me some blunt. I'll take him to a tavern. He's always much more agreeable when his breadbox is full."

"As are you." Jack gladly handed over a fistful of guineas. Now that his first mission was done, he was anxious to move on to Horse Guards, where his former military comrade had his offices. Closer study of Harriet's list the previous evening had sparked an idea.

❧

"Congratulations."

Harriet looked up from her dish of strawberry ice cream. She and Theo had deemed themselves deserving of a treat after spending yet another day making tedious morning calls, and so they had stopped at Gunter's Tea Shop on leaving Lady Merton's Grosvenor Square townhouse.

"Allow me to offer my felicitations on the happy news," continued Amirault, though his words were at odds with the accompanying smile. Like the stretch of perfect, pearly teeth it displayed, it had a certain hard-edged coldness.

"*Oui*, you are a very lucky lady," murmured Camille, who was accompanying him. "It is quite a coup, is it not, to have caught such a handsome, titled gentleman as Jack?"

Harriet's dislike of the Frenchwoman ratcheted up another notch. It was, she knew, unfair, perhaps. English society also saw marriage as a merging of material assets. And yet, something about Camille's slanted cat-like eyes and how they seemed always to be probing for a weakness put her back up.

"I was not fishing," she said pointedly.

"La, forgive me. My English is so very clumsy at times. It leaves much to be desired."

Harriet was quite sure that was a falsehood. Lies seemed to swath the Gallic beauty, fluttering around her like so many layers of gossamer silk.

"Lord Leete considers himself fortunate to have won Harriet's hand," piped up Theo in Harriet's defense. "They have much in common and make a very well-matched pair."

"Then they will no doubt have a very happy future together," replied Camille smoothly.

"Might we join you and Lady Thalia?" asked Amirault, indicating the pair of empty chairs at their table.

"Her name is *Theo*," announced Harriet.

"We seem to be putting—how do you English say it—our toes in our mouth," murmured Camille. "Perhaps we should move on before we give further offense."

Taking the oblique hint, Amirault remained standing. "I hope we may make amends by inviting you and your fiancé to attend a special private party at Vauxhall Gardens on Thursday evening, given by the Duc de Broilly." An infinitesimal pause. "And Lady Theo, too, of course. And we would, of course, be honored by your father's presence as well."

Quelling her irritation, Harriet responded with a polite nod. "Thank you. That sounds lovely. I am sure Jack will be delighted to be part of the gathering. Unfortunately, my father will not be available." It was the truth, though she would have lied if necessary. "He is in Portsmouth for the week on government business."

"What a pity." Amirault gave a resigned sigh. "I have heard so many people sing his praises, it would have been an honor to meet him."

"Perhaps some other time," said Harriet coolly.

"I shall look forward to it. But in the meantime, we shall have the pleasure of welcoming you and Leete—and Lady Theo. It will be a memorable evening, as there are gala fireworks planned, designed by the famous Austrian pyrotechnics expert, Herr Steuer, in honor of Wellington's latest successes in the Peninsula. And there will a number of interesting people in attendance, several of whom I am most anxious to have you meet."

"Oh?" said Harriet, raising an inquiring brow.

Amirault, however, went on smoothly, "By the by, Broilly is asking that all the guests come masked and costumed as a great British historical figure of the past in order to add to the festivities."

"I shall have trouble convincing Jack to don a powdered wig and silk stockings, but a simple domino may be possible. There is an old one belonging to my father in our attic that he can borrow." She looked to Camille. "Have you chosen someone, Madame La Rochelle?"

"I am thinking of Boudicca, the mythical Warrior Queen," replied Camille. "And you?"

"I must give it some thought." Harriet was about to turn back to the Comte when she noticed the oval pendant pinned to the Frenchwoman's bodice. Inside the gold filigree frame was a miniature portrait painted on ivory. "That is a lovely piece of art," she remarked. "Might I have a closer look?"

Camille came around the table. "It is my husband," she said softly.

"The detail is exquisite," said Harriet after taking several long moments to examine the delicately wrought brushstrokes.

Despite the small size, there was an undeniable magnetism to the fine-boned face. "He is a very handsome man."

Or was, amended Harriet to herself as she watched intently for any flicker of reaction from the Frenchwoman.

"It is a very good likeness." It might have been mere artifice that affected the tiny tremor in Camille's voice, but for an instant, it sounded heartfelt.

"Thank you, for allowing me a closer look," she said, feeling it would be churlish to keep staring, even though there was a mysterious power to the blue eyes that held her gaze.

"Come, Camille, we must be on our way," said Amirault, moving to her side and offering his arm. "Please excuse us, ladies. We are engaged to meet Lady Hillhouse for a pianoforte recital at the St. Alban's Musical Society."

"Yes, we must," said Camille in a small, sad voice, and let herself be led off without a further word.

"Fireworks give me a beastly headache," said Theo, once the front door had fallen shut. "I think I shall cry off."

"A trip to Vauxhall Gardens is always a raucous occasion, what with the noisy crowds, the free-flowing arrack punch, the dark pathways, and the whiff of forbidden pleasures hanging heavy as the scent of gunpowder in the night air," replied Harriet.

"It's not the sort of evening you enjoy either," commented Theo. "Why not demur as well?"

"I think Jack will want to attend," she answered evasively, unable to explain the real reason for her interest in Amirault and Camille.

"It is good of him to feel such loyalty to Madame La Rochelle," murmured her friend. She pushed aside her unfinished ice cream. "Though I am not sure she deserves it."

"Nor am I," confided Harriet. "However, unlike you, I do enjoy the booms and the brilliant explosions of sparks against the black velvet sky. So in spite of the company, it won't be an entirely unpleasant experience for me." She began rummaging in her reticule for her purse. "Sorry, but I had better return home. I've promised Jack that I shall drive out in the park with him this afternoon, and that entails yet another of Madame Deauville's stylish ensembles." A wry grimace. "I think I preferred being a drab country weed."

"No, no, we agreed it was time for the Wallflowers to turn over a new leaf!" Theo flashed a warm smile. "After a day of chattering tabbies, a breath of fresh air with Jack will be a lovely respite. The two of you have such a comfortable camaraderie. It bodes very well for a happy marriage. I am so very pleased for you. I... I think it is rare to find such a perfect match."

"Thank you." Harriet felt a guilty flush creep to her cheeks, wondering how in the name of Hades she was going to explain things when the sham engagement came to an end. But she forced herself to thrust aside such worries, deciding there were enough challenges to cope with at the present moment.

"It does seem to me," she went on softly, "that friendship must be at the heart of any meaningful relationship."

Their eyes met and Theo reached over to give her hand a small squeeze. "I couldn't agree more."

JACK HANDED Harriet up to the seat of his high-perch curricle. "Thank you for agreeing to drive out in the park at the fashionable hour. I know you dislike all these silly social rituals, but people expect it of a newly engaged couple, so we had best play along." He climbed up beside her and took hold of the reins. "And besides, I have some interesting information to pass on to you."

"As do I," she replied. "But let us hear your news first. I can see by your expression that you think it important."

"I do." A flick of his whip started the matched pair of bays trotting toward Rotten Row. "I got to thinking about all your research and cross-checking of documents, which ended up indicating Camille's husband was likely interred somewhere in Oxfordshire." Up ahead, a lumbering dray filled with hogsheads of ale suddenly swerved, forcing a quick maneuver to avoid careening into an oncoming barouche.

"So I visited my friend who is handling military intelligence at Horse Guards, and though it took some wheedling, I've managed to learn in exactly which towns prisoners of war are billeted."

"Bravo," she said. "Both for your cleverness, and for avoiding disaster back there. Thank Heaven you are a very skilled driver."

He grinned. "A compliment? I would swoon, but that would undo all my efforts to impress you."

"So," she mused, ignoring his quip, "we should be getting close to solving that part of the mystery."

"Yes. I've dispatched a Bow Street Runner to investigate. I'm told he's very good at what he does. If Pierre La Rochelle is there, we shall find him." Jack gave a sidelong glance, expecting another smile. Instead, he saw a pensive frown pinch at her profile.

"How will he recognize La Rochelle?" asked Harriet.

"You are developing a devious mind," he murmured. "Actually, I did think of that. Given the swirl of suspicions around all this, I gave the Runner a detailed physical description of Pierre."

Her face relaxed somewhat. "Excellent."

"We should hear within a matter of days. Assuming he's located, I shall journey there and have a long talk with my old friend."

"Before you inform Camille?"

Jack had asked himself the same question and wasn't sure of the answer. "I don't know yet," he admitted. "I shall make that decision when the time comes."

Harriet caught a lock of hair that the breeze had pulled free of her bonnet and tucked it behind her ear with an impatient little tug that drew an inward smile. Her subtle mannerisms—a look, a gesture, a tilt of her head—had become intimately familiar over the last few months. He was beginning to sense her moods before she spoke a word.

At the moment, there was an aura of anticipation thrumming from her body. She had something to tell him—something she felt was significant.

Her next words corroborated his guess.

"Perhaps you will have a better idea on what to do after Thursday evening,"

Jack waited for her to go on.

Harriet waited until the curricle had passed through the park gates and turned down one of the side carriageways before explaining, "Theo and I encountered Amirault and Camille at Gunter's. They invited us to a private party that's being given by the Duc de Broilly at Vauxhall Gardens in honor of Wellington's recent successes. There will be special fireworks, and we are asked to come in masquerade, as notable figures from British history."

"No velvet doublets or silk hose," he growled.

"I said as much. You can wear a simple domino. Remember the scarlet and black one you borrowed from Father when you and Wills attended the dowager Duchess of Sachem's Venetian breakfast? It is still in the attic here in London."

"If I must," he muttered. "But yes, it's an excellent opportunity for us to mingle with the French Royalists."

"Amirault mentioned that he has several people he wishes to introduce to us. Perhaps it was my imagination, but he had that sort of cat-in-the-cream pot look that bodes no good. I wonder what sort of surprise he has planned."

"Whatever it is, I will be ready for him," vowed Jack.

His hands tightened on the reins, mirroring the clench of his insides as he realized how very determined he was to shield Harriet from any threat. Their engagement might be a sham, but his feelings for her were very real. She had come to be very dear to him... no, that wasn't precisely right. She had been nestled somewhere in his heart for quite some time, a small flicker of warmth that had recently kindled to a bright flame.

No harm would be planned for them in the midst of a fancy party, he reminded himself. If danger was lurking elsewhere, he would have to be vigilant in keeping it well away from her.

The horses snorted and tossed their heads, pulling him back from such brooding thoughts.

Harriet shot him a quizzical look as the curricle lurched over the graveled pathway.

"Sorry," he said. "I was thinking about the Bow Street Runner. Perhaps, until this matter is resolved, I should hire one of his comrades to shadow your movements. Just as a precaution—"

"Absolutely not," she shot back. "It is entirely unnecessary."

Jack did not wish to alarm her by bringing up any reminder of the knife attack. And now that the first rush of worry had subsided, he agreed that he was overreacting. "Very well. But promise me you will not go out unaccompanied."

She hesitated, then gave a curt nod. "Fair enough."

Happy to have settled things so easily, he quickly returned to the topic of the masquerade party before she could change her mind.

"And what costume will you wear?"

"I have no idea." Harriet pursed her lips. "I am scheduled for another visit to Madame Deauville's shop on the morrow, in order to choose fabric for several more walking gowns. I shall ask her help in creating something suitably impressive."

"No doubt it will be. She is considered by all of London to be a magician with needle and thread."

The curricle slowed as they turned into Rotten Row, its wide expanse clogged with carriages. Stylish ladies and gentlemen strolled along the grassy verge, adding to the festive air of the haute monde parade. Jack drove for some moments in silence, very much aware of all the eyes turning on them.

Harriet shifted on the seat.

"It will all soon subside," he murmured. "Some new story or scandal will make them forget about us."

She sighed. "Yes, but it will likely be *us* who provide that new scandal."

Seeing her expression, he wondered if he had made a mistake in cajoling her into accepting his suggestion. At the time, it had seemed a reasonable one. But now, he was having misgivings.

But not, he admitted, because of the *ton* and its penchant for cruel gossip. The fact was, he enjoyed having Harriet as a constant company.

"Tell me something," she said abruptly. "Has Madame Deauville's swirls of silk and satin magically transformed *me*?"

Jack considered the question warily. There did not seem to be any good answer. He was damned if he said yes, and damned if he said no.

So what about simply saying the truth?

"Harry, you look absolutely splendid in all your new finery. The styles, the colors—and all the other little flourishes that a fellow can't put a name to—are magnificent. And you added some other indefinable element." He made a face. "Don't ask me what. I'm not a poet, so I can't begin to describe it."

A ripple stirred in the depth of her gaze.

"But dash it all, you've always appeared wonderful in my eyes. The furbelows and frills are all very well, however, for me, your essence is unchanged."

She blinked. Several times.

"So I'm the wrong person to ask," he muttered.

Harriet's expression went through a series of odd little contortions. But her only response was a single syllable.

"Oh."

Thankfully, a hail from a nearby carriage provided a welcome escape from the uncomfortable conversation. Jack turned and tipped his hat to the dowager Countess of Branford, an old school friend of his late grandmother.

"It's about time you settled down, you rapscallion," she said, reaching out to whack her cane against the curricle's painted wheel. "From what I have heard, the gel has enough sense—and enough starch—to keep you in line."

"Allow me to introduce, Miss Farnum," he said dryly.

The dowager raised her quizzing glass and regarded Harriet intently. "Aye, you'll do," she announced after a long moment. Jack thought he detected a flash behind the oversized glass lens. "Anyone who doesn't flinch from my scrutiny has some bottom." Another whack. "Come visit me, Miss Farnum and we'll have a talk about this knave."

"She likes playing the dragon," murmured Jack as the barouche moved on. "But her fire is quite harmless."

"Outspoken, opinionated ladies don't frighten me in the least," replied Harriet with a hint of humor. "I think I shall enjoy paying a call on her."

With that, their conversation moved on to the various social obligations that loomed in the coming week. The momentary awkwardness had passed, but as Jack looped down a quieter carriageway for the return trip to her townhouse, he couldn't help but note that though her tone was light, her mood seemed subdued.

Had he offended her? A lady liked to hear compliments, but somehow when he tried to hand them to Harriet, he turned into a clutch-fisted cawker.

They traded a few more casual comments concerning the people they had just seen, then lapsed into silence as the horses headed down half Moon Street.

Drawing to a halt, Jack jumped down from his perch and came around to assist her.

"Here, lad, " he tossed a coin to the young street-sweeper on the corner. "Come hold my team while I escort the lady inside."

It took several knocks to summon the butler to open the door.

"Your pardon, miss, but the footmen are moving some furniture away from the hearth in your father's study, as the chimney suddenly started smoking, and appears to require some repairs," explained Bailin in a harried voice. "I had better hurry back to make sure they don't make a hash of it."

"Of course," agreed Harriet. "We need not stand on ceremony with Lord Leete."

As Bailin rushed away, she undid her bonnet and set it on the sidetable.

Jack took a step closer, watching the tendrils of finespun hair at the nape of her neck begin to dance in a draft of air.

When she turned around, she seemed surprised to see him standing there. "Really, sir, you ought not to let your cattle take a chill."

Her pert mouth was somehow mere inches from his. Jack could see the enticing fullness of her lower lip, a soft, sweetly-shaped curve that sent a jolt of heat spiraling through his very bones.

He tried to reply, but the words seemed to catch in his throat. He couldn't speak.

He couldn't think. Which explained why, as the air squeezed from his lungs, he lowered his head...

How long the kiss—if kiss it was—went on was impossible to gauge. Minutes? Hours? All Jack knew was that Harriet looked as dazed as he felt when at last their lips feathered apart.

"Sorry," he rasped. "I don't know what came over me."

"Y-You are overset by all this. I-I have heard that the specter of a legshackle can do that to a gentleman," she stammered.

Jack let out a wry chuckle. "If anyone should be overset, it is you, Harry." He kept his hands resting on her shoulders, simply because it felt good to do so. She didn't try to pull away.

"Ah, but you know me. Steady as a brick."

A very unbrick-like warmth radiated up through the layers of fabric to caress his palms. "Shall you never let me live down that remark?"

A smile curled at the corners of her mouth, and it was all he could do to keep from kissing her again. "I haven't decided."

"Wretch," he replied, returning the smile. It was only with great reluctance that he shuffled his feet and let his hands fall away. "I've arranged to meet Jamie at White's, so I had better take my leave. We're going on to rendezvous with a friend of his who is working on finding Verdunne."

"Be careful," said Harriet, an unreadable flicker clouding her gaze for a moment.

"I will," promised Jack. "My friend at Horse Guards has also arranged a meeting with some of my old military comrades in Kent who are involved in overseeing the handling of French prisoners on parole here in England. So I will be leaving at first light tomorrow and will likely not return until just before the party at Vauxhall Gardens."

He couldn't keep from reaching out and brushing a curl from her cheek. "So you must vow to be careful as well."

"I told you, I will not go out alone, if that makes you feel better."

"It does," he replied.

"My only engagement is a trip to Madame Deauville's shop. And the only threat there is to Father's purse." She gave a rueful grimace. "Her creations are hideously expensive."

"But worth every farthing," murmured Jack. "However, if she decides to dress you as Queen Elizabeth, please promise me you won't dye your glorious hair red."

"No red," agreed Harriet.

"Excellent." Jack backed toward the door. "Until Thursday, then."

"Yes, until Thursday."

CHAPTER 16

A kiss? Harriet pursed her lips as the carriage rolled along the cobbled street toward the dressmaker's shop. She had lain awake half the night puzzling over the fleeting encounter. *Had Jack really meant to kiss her? Or...*

She couldn't seem to think of an alternative. It had definitely felt like a kiss. A tremor had tingled through her as their lips touched, and she could have sworn that she had felt him react as well.

And he had called her mouse-brown hair glorious.

"Oooh, how exciting," murmured her maid.

Harriet looked up, a guilty flush stealing to her cheeks. Were her schoolgirl reveries written that plainly on her face?

"A masquerade party, under the midnight stars," went on Ellie, much to Harriet's relief. "How romantic."

"Not really," she replied dryly. "There will be a crush of people crowding the gardens, and fireworks booming and sparking loud as cannonfire."

"Yes, but darkness always adds a cloak of intrigue," said Ellie with a soft sigh. "And you will be able to look at Lord Leete's handsome face bathed in silvery moonlight."

"It is a masquerade, remember? Lord Leete's face will be completely covered," pointed out Harriet.

Her maid looked a little crestfallen but quickly recovered. "Well, perhaps you will be surprised. I still say it could be wildly romantic."

"Perhaps," she allowed.

Ellie's vivid imagination was soon satisfied as Mrs. McNulty and her assistants quickly got into the spirit of fashioning a striking costume for the duc's party.

"I think we should choose a queen," said the dressmaker after considering the rolls of sumptuous fabric stacked in the corner of the fitting room. "That way we get to work with all the glitter and pomp of royalty. The question is which one. I should not like to portray you as a widget or featherhead."

"I suggest Queen Caroline of Ansbach, consort of George I," offered Mrs. Currough, who had paused in the corridor to peek through the gap in the draperies. "She was known for her grace and intelligence, and assembled a fascinating court of thinkers and artists at Kensington Palace."

"Excellent! Come, girls, let us get to work." Mrs. McNulty clapped her hands together, then barked out a flurry of orders that sent her assistants scurrying for gold braid, silver thread and baskets of creamy lace and jeweltone fringing.

"What is the occasion?" asked Mrs. Currough.

"A masquerade party tomorrow in Vauxhall Gardens, given by the Duc de Broilly," answered Harriet. "Lord Leete and I have been invited by Comte Amirault and Madame La Rochelle."

A pensive frown passed over the Irish Beauty's face. "Amirault and La Rochelle," she repeated. "I have heard those two names spoken of recently." After a long moment of thought, her shoulders lifted in a shrug. "But I can't place where. It doesn't matter, of course. It's simply that I wouldn't have expected you and Leete to be acquainted with the French community here in London."

"Madame La Rochelle and Leete formed a friendship while he was a prisoner of the French army in the Peninsula."

Mrs. Currough's frown flickered back for an instant. "From what I hear, the French community is a hornet's nest of warring factions and duplicitous intrigue. I am sure you and Leete need no counsel from me, however..."

She paused, fixing Harriet with a concerned look. "We women of the demimonde talk among ourselves. Men's tongues tend to loosen after an evening of wine and pleasure, and so my friends are privy to many secrets. I would simply say that if I were you, I would be very careful about being drawn into their tangle of affairs."

"Leete is of the same opinion," answered Harriet carefully.

Mrs. Currough's expression brightened. "Then let us speak of more pleasant things." She moved to the bolts of rich fabrics. "I would recommend that lovely gold-threaded seafoam green brocade for the underdress of your costume gown. A layer of sarcenet..."

The next hour passed in a bustle of cutting and pinning, as patterns were made and trimmings were chosen.

"La, you will look even more regal than a queen when I am done," said Mrs. McNulty as she brandished a sewing needle and a handful of glittering paste jewels.

"I am sure I won't recognize myself tomorrow evening," quipped Harriet.

"That, my dear, is the whole point of a masquerade."

CLIMBING QUICKLY up to the perch of his curricle, Jack turned the horses for the main road and urged them to as fast a pace as the gusting rain allowed. With the masquerade party looming in the evening, he was anxious to return to London as quickly as possible. Yesterday, fearing that his morning meeting might be lengthy, he had sent a message to Harriet, arranging to meet her at the main entrance to the Vauxhall Gardens rather than calling for her at her residence. But given what he had just discovered, he did not like the idea of leaving her alone amidst the crowd of revelers.

The scribbled notes tucked inside his oilskin cloak, made during the lengthy interviews with several military officers involved with overseeing French prisoners in England, had only increased his misgivings about Camille. He was sure she was lying about Pierre being missing, and yet he could come up with no reason for it.

Which in itself set off warning bells in his head. An unpredictable enemy was dangerous.

Strange how he had come to see her as an enemy. A few short weeks ago, he had fancied himself in thrall to her seductive beauty, her winsome charm. Or rather, he had been in thrall to the Camille he had fashioned from memory and longing. An imaginary ideal, no more real than a figure cut out of pasteboard.

Perhaps the image had crumbled because in contrast to the steady friendship and forthright honesty of Harriet, the French-woman's allure was no more substantial than dust.

Love was more than a flirtatious smile, a throaty laugh. He knew that now.

The wind tore at his cloak, the rain lashed his face, sending icy rivulets snaking down his spine. And yet Jack was aware of an elemental warmth centered in his core.

Harriet.

He loved Harriet. In that storm-dark moment, it hit him with all the force of a thunderclap. At heart, he had known it for ages. It had simply taken time for the realization to penetrate his thick skull.

A crack of his whip drew a little more speed from the horses. There was no cause for alarm, he assured himself. But his nerves were on edge, and some primitive protective instinct had kicked up to drum an urgent tattoo inside his head.

And he had learned long ago to trust his instincts.

ELLIE DID up the last fastening of the gown and stepped back with an admiring gasp. "Oooh, Miss Harriet, You look like a fairytale princess!" She picked up the paste-jeweled crown from the dressing table and held it up to the light. "What a pity you have to spoil the effect of all this lovely glitter with a black silk mask that hides half your face."

"I think I have more than enough glitter," said Harriet, doing a slow twirl in front of the cheval glass. The gold-threaded fabric sparked like live fire, setting off winks of light along the faux-emerald encrusted trimmings. Mrs. McNulty and her seamstresses had outdone themselves in creating a costume fit for a queen. It was all make-believe, of course, but at the moment she felt rather regal.

Would Jack notice how well the gown complemented her curves?

Chiding herself for such silly schoolgirl longings, Harriet fluffed up her skirts one last time and then turned away from her reflection. Romance had no place in her thoughts. This was purely business. They had a mystery to solve.

"I will wait until it's time to leave before putting on the crown," she told her maid. Meanwhile, there was a detailed map of Oxfordshire in her father's study which she wanted to consult. An idea had popped into her head just now while she was dressing, and it wouldn't take long to see if it was worth mentioning to Jack this evening. "I need to take a quick look at something in Father's study."

Ellie followed her down the corridor, clucking in disapproval.

"But there's repair work being done on the chimney. You might get soot on the hem of that gorgeous confection."

"The garden grounds aren't exactly pristine," pointed out Harriet.

A sniff, followed by a sigh. "Yes, but we want Lord Leete to see you in all your glory," said Ellie. "Is he coming dressed as a prince?"

Harriet chuckled as she reached for the door latch of the study. "No, he is going to wear Father's old red and black domino. I had it delivered to his townhouse."

Her maid made a horrified face. "But that will clash with your colors!"

"Alas, a prince was above my power of persuasion. It was all I could do to convince him to wear any costume at all."

"That's not very romantic," said Ellie, repeating a sentiment she had been voicing before.

"I may have to curtail your reading of Mrs. Radcliffe's novels. They seem to be giving you overdramatic ideas of romance," replied Harriet dryly.

"But romance is all about drama," objected Ellie. "And passion."

Harriet raised her brows. "I won't ask what you know about passion."

That drew a flustered flush. "I had better go give the crown a last polishing and lay out the hairpins," she said quickly and scuttled back toward Harriet's rooms.

Repressing a smile, Harriet pushed open the study room. There *was* a lot of dust, she saw, and the workman had been a little sloppy in laying down a covering on the oaken floor. Skirting around a scattering of ashes, she headed for the massive pearwood desk set by the bank of windows, then slowed in consternation on seeing papers and documents strewn in a jumble atop the leather blotter. Her father was meticulous about keeping his work in order...

"Pray, what are you doing down there?" she demanded of the figure crouched between the desk and door leading out to the back terrace.

"Sweeping up, Miss," came the raspy reply.

"You ought to start by the hearth," she said sternly, "before the draft blows the dust over the books and papers."

"Aye, miss."

Harriet waited, intent on not letting the lazy knave shirk his duties.

He continued to shuffle around on his hands and knees.

Shifting slightly, she saw that one of the desk drawers was ajar. It wasn't one that was normally kept locked. Still, the back of her neck began to prickle. She took a step closer and saw he had no hand broom.

"Just how are you sweeping? By conjuring the motes of dust into a bin across that room with the flick of a magic wand?"

"I was just fetching a tool that had fallen, Miss," he whined, holding up a thin-bladed chisel. "I mean to start sweeping right away."

"Get up," she commanded.

He rose, head down, shoulders hunched, and started to sidle around to the hearth.

"Stay where you are, and tell me what you were doing down there."

"Just my job, miss." He finally looked up and cast her a beseeching look through his gold-tipped lashes. "Please, I have a sick mother and grandmother to support. I cannot afford to lose this job."

Harriet drew in a sharp inhale as their eyes met.

"Please," he repeated, a hopeful smile curling on his well-shaped mouth. He was an extremely handsome man, so no doubt he was used to wheedling favors from females.

Moving back a step, she braced a hand on the bookshelf,

considering the plea. "Look around you. Your work is unacceptable."

His eyes lowered to the floor in contrition. "I promise I shall do better."

As he spoke, Harriet calmly opened the lid of the rosewood box beneath her fingers and drew out her father's pistol. "That won't be necessary."

Drawing a bead on his chest, she added, "*Alors*, Colonel La Rochelle—your wife appears to be expending a great deal of time and tears trying to locate you. As is your old friend Jack. And yet, here you are, safe and sound, in my father's townhouse. Would you care to explain that?"

La Rochelle opened his mouth to speak, then seemed to change his mind. Tugging his grimy jacket into place, he slowly straightened to his full height. "It would seem that prevarication is pointless. Tell me, how did you know it was me?"

"It is I who am asking the questions, sir. And I expect some answers."

He lifted his shoulders in a graceful shrug.

"And so will Jack." The Frenchman's *sang froid* was making her blood boil. "What a miserable, cowardly act to try to murder a friend. You should be ashamed of yourself."

"Jack is a soldier. He knows that in time of war, personal feelings cannot interfere with a mission."

"What mission?" she demanded. "And why draw him in to whatever sordid plot you had planned."

La Rochelle picked at a loose thread on his cuff. "It was an unfortunate accident that Camille encountered him outside the gaming hell. We thought perhaps he could be used to our advantage." His smile turned half mocking. "But you know what a highly developed sense of honor he has. Not only did he refuse to introduce Camille to your father, but he undertook to find me, which was a great inconvenience."

"An inconvenience which called for cold-blooded murder?"

The Frenchman's expression remained neutral. "Verdunne exceeded his orders. He was only ordered to have his ruffians wound Jack, but he's always never much liked Englishmen, especially now that your armies have our Emperor on the run."

"So, you are loyal to Napoleon?"

Another shrug. "I am loyal to whatever side will hold power in France."

Appalled, Harriet pressed for more information. "I don't understand. Why are you here in England?"

"To make sure I make myself valuable to whichever Royalist faction will emerge as triumphant. The documents which your father possesses list the names of those men both here and in France who will be favored by the British government. That will prove invaluable to me and my associates."

"You are working with Amirault?"

La Rochelle heaved a bored sigh. "Enough questions, mademoiselle. Are you going to shoot me?"

"I should, but I daresay Jack will have a good many more queries to make of you." Harriet gestured with the pistol at the desk chair. "Sit." Her eyes shifted for just an instant as she looked for the bell, in order to ring for the footmen to come truss up her prisoner.

A mistake. Seizing his chance, La Rochelle kicked the chair over, knocking her back against the bookshelves. With the same cat-like quickness, he spun around and slammed his shoulder against the terrace door, bursting the lock. A split second later he had disappeared into the shrubbery.

Cursing herself for a fool, Harriet replaced the pistol in the box. No sense in raising the alarm, she decided. Bailin and the footmen were no match for La Rochelle, even if they could catch up to him. There was also the chance that they would not allow her to go on to Vauxhall Gardens, and that might ruin whatever strategy Jack had planned for the evening.

She needed to leave soon, so as to be sure not to keep Jack

waiting at the entrance… and after a moment of further reflection, it seemed doubtful La Rochelle would try to return anytime soon, so she simply closed up the back door, and straightened up her father's desk before heading back to her room.

"Oh, Miss—you've gone and mussed up all the beautiful folds!" exclaimed Ellie.

"Never mind the folds," said Harriet. She was about to wave off the crown as well, but then thought better of it. Jack might well want to mingle at the party as if nothing alarming had happened, and so she ought to be in full costume, including the black mask that was part of her headgear. Reluctantly taking a seat at her dressing table, she submitted to her maid's ministrations.

But as the minutes seemed to pass slowly as hours, her patience began to fray. "Oh, do hurry with that dratted crown.

"Then stop squirming," muttered Ellie. She thrust in the last few pins, then hastily gathered up their cloaks. "Now we are ready to be off."

~

"WHAT THE DEVIL…" Jack stared in consternation at the clothing strewn around his dressing room.

"I only discovered it just now, milord. None of the staff heard any sounds or saw any signs of an intruder," said his valet apologetically. "I haven't noted anything of value missing, but I shall, of course, make a thorough examination."

Jack surveyed the mess. "That can wait. First of all, find that blasted domino and be quick about it."

"Er, that is the one item that seems to be gone, sir."

He spun around. "*Gone?*"

"Yes, milord. Though why a thief would take it is beyond me."

There could only be one explanation. Harriet had somehow put herself in danger.

Uttering a curse, Jack rushed to his sitting room and retrieved a small pocket pistol from his desk drawer. "Summon my carriage," he ordered as he shoved the weapon into his pocket. His curricle team was too winded to continue on to Vauxhall Gardens. "NOW!"

As his valet pelted off, he threw off his oilskin cloak and grabbed up a dark overcoat. The clouds had scudded off during his journey from Kent, leaving a clear sky. *A good night for fireworks.* Though he feared that the real bang and spark would be playing out on the grounds of the gardens.

His chest clenched. Harriet was alone and unprotected—

"Why is your household racing around like bats flying out of hell?" asked James as he entered the room.

"Because there is a devil on the loose." Jack grabbed his friend's arm. "Is your carriage right outside?"

"Yes—"

"Then let us fly. I'll explain on the way."

"ELLIE, listen carefully. Instead of coming with me, I want you to return home immediately and have Bailin and the footmen guard the house against any intruders," said Harriet as their coachman drew the horses to a halt near the entrance to the Grand Walk. "I will explain later, but for now, just do as I say."

"But, Miss Harriet! You can't be left on your own here, with all the tussle and bustle of unsavory strangers," protested her maid. "It's too dangerous."

Squaring her mask with an impatient tug, Harriet glanced out the carriage window and saw the familiar red and black glimmer of her father's old domino through the smoky haze of the torchlight.

"Look, Lord Leete is already waiting for me," she pointed out, feeling a rush of relief that he was there. "With only a short stretch to cross, I'm not going to come to any grief."

"Very well, then," said Ellie, after reassuring herself that Jack was indeed standing in the recess of the archway. She unlatched the door, allowing Harriet to descend to the graveled walkway.

A gust ruffled her skirts, drawing a number of raucous catcalls. Hunching her shoulders, she tried to hurry her steps, but all around her, the masked revelers were pushing and jostling, their overloud voices already slurred by spirits. She craned her neck, trying to see Jack through the swaying headcoverings and bobbing plumes. But he seemed to have been swallowed up in the crowd.

Quelling a flutter of nerves, Harriet made herself keep moving. He had to be just ahead.

Her heavy skirts tangled around her legs and her heeled shoes were slipping and sliding awkwardly over the sharp stones. She tried to angle across to the perimeter of the path, but a sudden shove from behind sent her stumbling.

A black-gloved hand caught hold of her arm, keeping her upright.

Twisting around, she was about to cry out when she saw it was the red and black domino looming close to her face.

"Jack!" she exclaimed. "Thank God."

He gestured her to silence with a quick touch of his finger to her lips. The crush of the crowd carried them through the entrance. His stride lengthened and Harriet found herself struggling to keep pace. The noise, the revelers, the wildly flickering lanterns all added to her sense of confusion. Her breathing was coming in ragged gasps and all at once she was feeling a little dizzy and disoriented.

"Please, we need to find a quiet spot to stop and talk for a moment," she said with low urgency. "I have much to tell you."

His only reaction was to move even faster. Somewhere close by, a loud boom rent the air. One of the attractions at the end of the Great Walk was a mock sea battle, and it seemed that the cannons had begun to fire.

Though her head was reeling, Harriet was familiar enough with the layout of the gardens to know that the battle was at the opposite end of the Gardens from where the duc's private party was being held.

"Jack!" She dug in her heels. The crowds had thinned somewhat and there seemed no reason they couldn't slow down and talk.

At last, he responded. But not as Harriet expected. Pulling her close, he bent low, as if to murmur in her ear. It was then that she felt the prick of cold steel touch against her neck.

"Come along quietly, mademoiselle." Though low and muffled, the voice was unmistakably that of La Rochelle. "Or I'll be forced to ensure your silence."

There were people all around, and the light from the lanterns cast a bright illumination over the walkway. "You wouldn't dare," said Harriet, trying to sound braver than she felt.

"You think anyone will notice me carrying a drunken woman into the bushes?" he shot back. "You are naïve, mademoiselle. Now come along. I won't ask again."

Boom! Boom! Boom! The cannons were firing more rapidly, much to the glee of the spectators, who were watching great puffs of smoke float up above the trees.

Harriet realized he was right. Struggling would be foolish. Until she knew what was going on, it was best to do as she was told.

She let her muscles go limp.

"A wise decision." Keeping his arm wrapped tightly around her waist, La Rochelle once again quickened his steps. They passed a small pavilion, its pale marble columns painted in silvery moonlight, then he suddenly turned down one of the infamous Dark Walks, unlit footpaths which were known for attracting only people who were up to no good.

CHAPTER 17

*P*ounding his fist against his palm in frustration, Jack glanced yet again out the carriage window. "Can't your coachman manage more than a snail's pace?"

"The road is clogged with revelers," said James. He twisted a brass latch on a storage compartment and drew out a carriage pistol. "You should have told me about these new developments sooner. I would have kept a closer eye on the ladies while you were away."

"It was all too vague. I had nothing but nebulous suspicions," answered Jack. "But I should have anticipated the worst. Now Harriet..." His throat suddenly tightened too much to go on.

"We'll find her." James checked the priming of his weapon, then slipped it in his coat pocket. "Are you sure Theo is not attending the party?"

"Yes. She did not accompany Harriet to have a costume made, so she would have nothing to wear."

His friend nodded grimly. "Good. Then we may concentrate all our efforts on finding Harriet."

Jack twitched at the drapery, refusing to think about what to do if they didn't. "Bloody hell," he growled, suddenly rising from the seat. "It will be faster to go on from here on foot."

James followed him out the door, and they began weaving in and out among the snorting horses and jostling vehicles. Up ahead, the torches around the entrance lit the night with a reddish glow. *An ominous omen?* Quelling a spurt of fear, Jack started to run.

Ignoring the curses of the coachmen, he dodged stomping hooves and bumping wheels, his boots crunching over the rutted gravel as he rounded a lumbering barouche.

A whip cracked. Veering sharply to avoid the lash, Jack stumbled up against an oncoming carriage. Moonlight played over the lacquered trim and brass, illuminating the familiar decorative trim.

"Lord Leete!" gasped Harriet's maid as she cracked open the door. "B-but how can that be? We saw you waiting—"

"Where?" he demanded.

"Right at the main entrance. Harriet recognized the red and black domino."

James skidded to a stop just in time to catch the maid's words. "They can't have gone far," he wheezed.

Jack didn't bother pointing out that a spiderweb of dark, twisting pathways ran through the sprawling Gardens. If Harriet were a captive, they could search all night and not find her. He didn't even know what costume—

"What is she wearing?" he asked.

Ellie quickly described Harriet's gown and mask.

It was a very thin thread on which to hang his hopes. He could only pray it wouldn't snap.

"We haven't a moment to lose," he said to James.

"Miss Harriet ordered me to return home and have Bailin lock up the house," said the maid in some confusion.

"Do so," he ordered. Seeing the fear on Ellie's face, he added. "I won't allow any harm come to her." A rash promise, but he meant to keep it.

Slamming the door shut, he spun around and grabbed his friend's arm. "Follow me."

~

BRANCHES SNAGGED ON HER SKIRTS, jagged yew needles scraped her face as La Rochelle dragged Harriet through a narrow opening in the trees and into a small pleasure pavilion. A latch clicked shut, and a lantern flared to life.

Choking back her fear, she fought for breath as she finally managed to pull off her mask and attached tiara.

"Sit down, Miss Farnam." Camille motioned with a golden arrow to the single stool set in the center of the small space. She was dressed in a flowing white tunic, fastened at the waist with a jewel-studded belt. A quiver filled with more golden missiles hung at her hip.

"The persona of Boudicca, the Warrior Queen, suits you well," said Harriet, making no move to do as she was told. "But if you recall history, Boudicca was defeated soundly."

"You have a clever tongue, Miss Farnum," replied Camille. She dropped the arrow and pulled a slim dagger from the quiver. "Too clever. You've created a great deal of trouble by disrupting our plans. Now, you shall help make amends."

"Put the weapon away," counseled Amirault, who stepped out from the shadows behind her. "I am sure Miss Farnum will see reason without us resorting to unpleasantness."

Harriet quickly glanced around. There were no others present. But three against one did not offer good odds for extricating herself from this coil, she thought wryly.

"What is it you want from me?" she asked as calmly as she could.

"Information," said Amirault with poisonous politeness.

"Pierre was hoping to obtain the list of names we need from your father's study. But as Camille pointed out, you interfered yet again. However, we know you serve as hostess and occasional scribe for your father. It seems likely you have in your head what we need."

"You are mistaken," answered Harriet. It was the truth. Her father took his responsibilities very seriously and did not share confidential government matters with anyone.

"I think you are lying," said Camille, her blue eyes reflecting the dancing lantern flame as she took a step closer.

"Do not make this difficult, mademoiselle," said Pierre. "You will be released unharmed as soon as you tell us what we need to know. And then, *voila*—we may all forget this unfortunate interlude."

She doubted that she was meant to leave the room alive. After all, Pierre and his wife hadn't flinched at conspiring to murder Jack.

Jack. Looking down, Harriet thought furiously on how to draw out the questioning. That Jack would be able to find her was unlikely—the Gardens were too vast, and he hadn't a clue as to what had happened. But surrendering to despair, and the manipulative wiles of Camille, caused the taste of bile to rise in her throat. No matter how hopeless, she meant to fight to the end.

"Why do you need the list of important Royalists?" she queried.

"To talk and perhaps deal—" began Amirault.

"To eliminate those who stand in the way of us emerging as the leaders of the new monarchist government in France," interrupted Camille. "The Bourbon heir to the throne is weak. The real power will lie with his advisors."

"And you see your husband and Comte Amirault as filling those roles?"

"But of course."

"That seems a rather cold-blooded means of achieving your goals," said Harriet. "I confess, I find it hard to understand how you could have allowed an attack on Jack, given the special friendship that had developed between you. He credits you with saving his life through your kindness and compassion."

"Friendship! *Alors*, poor Jack. His sense of English nobility makes him very naïve. My caring for him was simply because we decided that having the heir to an English earldom as a grateful friend could prove useful if the fortunes of war turned against Napoleon. But when dear Jack proved too honorbound to help me with my plans, he became a liability rather than an asset."

Harriet couldn't repress a shiver of disgust. "I would call you a snake, but that would be maligning reptiles."

Anger blazed in Camille's eyes. The dagger was still in her hand and she jabbed it perilously close to Harriet's face. "I suggest you swallow your insults and turn your tongue to telling us what we want to know. And quickly."

TAKING the steps two at a time, Jack raced up to the private terrace overlooking the Grove, which had been reserved for the duc's party. A footman in livery tried to block his entrance, but he pushed him aside and headed for the center of the marble-tiled expanse.

James hurried after him, leaving a trail of mud on the pristine white stone.

Silently cursing the fancy masks, Jack turned in a slow circle, trying to spot Camille or Amirault.

"Lord Leete?" An elegant lady in an elaborate Georgian gown and plumed headdress approached. "Lord Osborne? Is something amiss?"

Jack recognized Mrs. Currrough's voice. "Have you seen Mrs.

La Rochelle and Comte Amirault?" he demanded without preamble.

She came closer and answered softly. "I noticed an urchin sneak through the balusters and whisper something to the Comte. A few minutes later, he left with a lady. I could not tell who it was."

"How long ago?"

"Ten minutes, no more."

He hesitated, exchanging a worried look with James. There were few options left, and none of them were good.

"Is Harriet in trouble?" asked the Irish Beauty.

"I fear Amirault is holding her captive somewhere here in the Gardens," he replied tersely. "But I haven't a clue as to where to begin looking."

She fisted her hands in her skirts. "I may be able to help. A friend of mine in the demimonde occasionally consorts with men of Amirault's circle. There is a small pleasure pavilion hidden close to the Dark Walk that they favor for their revelries."

Hope flared in Jack's chest. "Can you describe where it is?"

"Better than that, I can show you to the pathway."

He took her arm. "Then lead the way—as fast as your feet will carry you."

"I'VE TOLD YOU, I know nothing," said Harriet, parrying yet another question.

Amirault expelled a mournful sigh. It was clear her interrogators were losing patience. "Alas, I find that hard to believe. We have spoken to a great many people about your father, and it is said he has the utmost respect for your judgment and intelligence."

Harriet didn't feel very smart at the moment. She should have been more careful. "My father may give me credit for possessing a brain, but that does not mean he shares government secrets with me." Though she knew it was unwise, she couldn't help but add, "Unlike the three of you, he is a man of honor and integrity. He does not betray his oath of allegiance."

"Honor is a pitiful notion for lackwits and fools." Camille brandished the dagger. "As you are about to learn."

"I think not," came a low voice from out of the gloom.

Harriet hardly dared to believe her ears.

Camille whirled around, then gave a light laugh as she saw Jack step from the shadows. "What do you intend to do, *cheri?* Shoot me?"

"If need be," came the calm answer.

The Frenchwoman's face betrayed a spasm of surprise as he raised his weapon. She hesitated for an instant, then made a lunge to grab Harriet.

A *bang* reverberated off the walls and, for an instant, a shower of sparks lit the sliver of steel slowly spinning into the shadows.

As Camille cried out and clutched her bleeding hand to her breast, La Rochelle started to draw a pistol from inside his coat, but suddenly froze as James appeared from the shadows and touched a gun barrel to the back of his skull. "I, too, will have no compunction about pulling the trigger." A metallic click punctuated the warning. "So drop your weapon."

Slanting a murderous look at Jack, La Rochelle did as he was ordered.

Shaking off her initial shock, Camille attempted a tearful plea. "Surely you must know that Miss Farnum was never in real danger, *cheri.* I confess, we were trying to frighten her into talking just now." Her lashes fluttered as she essayed a tentative smile. "The misunderstandings will all be explained if we can simply discuss this like friends—"

"We are not friends," said Jack coolly. "Your charm has worn thin, my dear. It is clear we never were."

Camille's gaze narrowed and her bleeding fingers tightened into a fist.

Harriet didn't give a fig for the reaction of the Frenchwoman or her compatriots. She was only aware of Jack, and the flare of firebright emotion in his eyes.

Amirault's look of shock slowly turned to a cynical smile. "Well, well. It seems we have lost a chance at winning a victory. But the game is simply a stalemate, not a loss," he said. "You cannot turn us over to the authorities for abducting Miss Farnum without exposing her to some very unpleasant gossip. Her reputation would be utterly ruined. And since you cannot prove any other crime against us..."

He lifted his shoulders in a self-satisfied Gallic shrug. "Come, Pierre, let us take Camille away and see to her injury."

"The three of you won't be going anywhere." The door flew open and Beaumont, his mask tipped back to reveal a grim look of satisfaction on his handsome face, stepped aside to let four men enter. They too were in masks and costumes, but quickly revealed themselves to be no ordinary revelers.

"You three will be leaving here, but only to make the journey to Newgate prison," announced the man dressed as Richard the Lion-Hearted. His sword might have been made of pasteboard, but the pistol he drew was quite real. "As head of Foreign Office intelligence, my men and I are authorized to place you under arrest. Monsieur Beaumont alerted us that there might be trouble at the duc's party tonight, and when we saw Lord Leete and Lord Osborne leave so abruptly, we followed."

"They heard everything, Amirault," added Beaumont. "I've long suspected you meant to use nefarious means to gain control of our Royalist cause, but murder?"

The next few minutes passed by in a blur. Harriet was only dimly aware of the prisoners being secured and marched away. All her thoughts were on the warm, hard press of Jack's muscled arms around her, the faint stubbling of whiskers along the line of his jaw, the possessive press of his lips.

A kiss? This time, there was no room for doubt. The intensity of it had all her senses reeling. Holding him close, she abandoned herself to the sweet sensation of his mouth, and all the glorious things it was doing to hers.

If only...

If only it would last for more than a fleeting interlude.

Jack broke off the embrace with a ragged sigh. "I—I thought I had lost you," he whispered. And then to her surprise, his lips feathered over her brow, her cheeks and came to rest on the tiny hollow at the base of her throat.

Her pulse began to quicken, spreading a sweet heat to chase away the fear lingering in her limbs.

It was a long moment before he slowly raised his head. "Those varlets didn't harm you in any way, did they?"

"The only injury I suffered is a bruise to my pride," answered Harriet, as she smoothed her fingers through his wind-snarled hair. "What a fool I was—I should have known as soon as he touched me that it wasn't you."

"It's me who's the fool," said Jack. "I never imagined my friends—my former friends—were capable of such evil."

"That's because you are, at heart, such a good and honorable man."

His arms tightened around her. "God knows, I have my faults and weaknesses. Too many to count."

"That's just as well. I'm not very good at mathematics."

A chuckle stirred deep in his throat. "What a corker—I know for a fact that you are prodigiously skilled in doing all sorts of complicated calculations."

And yet, Harriet wanted to say, the only equation she cared about was exceedingly simple—one plus one equals two. Instead, she merely murmured. "It was a devilishly difficult conundrum to solve. There's no need to tally up mistakes. We both made them."

"But one of mine put you in mortal danger," countered Jack. "Can you ever forgive me?"

She buried her face in the collar of his coat, reveling in the comfortable feel of his closeness.

"What are you thinking?" he asked softly.

"Just that..." She didn't intend to go on, but the words seemed to have a will of their own. "Just that it seems as if I fit perfectly into the chiseled contours of your body, all the hard and soft edges melding together so well that it is hard to tell them apart." Embarrassed at how it sounded aloud, she added, "It's a silly thought, brought on, no doubt, by an excess of emotion."

Jack hugged her closer. "I don't find it a silly thought at all. I was thinking much the same thing."

"Were you really?"

"Yes. And here is what was foremost in my mind." He released his hold and slowly tipped up her chin. Their eyes met for an instant, and then his mouth gently touched hers. "You are so sweetly soft while I am all rough edges. And yet, when I kiss you, the differences seem to disappear. Like so..."

"Ah," said Harriet when after a lengthy interlude he lifted his lips. "That was a very thorough explanation." She reached up to caress the tip of his chin. "Just so you know, I like your rough edges."

"And I like all your nuanced softness—your silky hair, your velvety skin," Jack pressed his cheek to hers. "I even like the brick-like bumps I get when we butt heads."

"I can be very hard-headed," she said.

"Delightfully so."

Harriet laughed, but before she could respond, a discreet cough interrupted the exchange.

"Forgive me for intruding on this private moment, but Mr.

Farraday of the Foreign Office and his men have taken away the prisoners," said James. "And so I was wondering whether you intend to stay here all night whispering endearments to each other? Or would you like to return to Mayfair in the comfort of my carriage?"

"The Dark Walk was made for stolen kisses," murmured Jack. "But much as I would like to linger, I am sure Harriet has seen quite enough of Vauxhall Gardens for now. And we ought to inform our households that all's well that ends well."

She would have been quite happy to stay in his arms until dawn, however, Jack's dry humor did remind her that Ellie and Bailin would be very worried.

"Yes, we had better go," she agreed.

"Excellent," said James, stomping his muddy boots as he turned. "My feet were getting awfully cold out there."

They quickly made their way clear of the dark trees and emerged on the Grand Walk. James tactfully forged ahead, leaving Harriet and Jack some privacy to follow along at their own pace. Overhead, the diamond-bright winking of the stars was suddenly highlighted by a burst of colorful sparks as the gala fireworks display began.

Jack looked up, the trailing glitter of fire gilding his profile. "We have much to celebrate."

"Indeed," she replied, though heading for home was a bitter-sweet reminder that with the mystery solved, she and Jack would have no real reason to be spending time together in the future.

To mask her plummeting spirits, Harriet quickly added a light quip. "The festivities are quite spectacular tonight. I am almost sorry that we are not attending the duc's party." She fluffed her jewel-trimmed skirts, which were now a little worse for wear. "It's not that I am in the mood for frivolities, but it's a pity to waste Madame Deauville's magnificent costume."

Jack twitched a faint smile, yet his expression took on an odd little pinch. He walked on in silence for several strides before replying. "As to that, we could have a masquerade ball to celebrate our wedding."

Her heart spun in a slow, dizzying circle within her ribcage. "But you didn't really ask me to marry you. We agreed that I am supposed to cry off."

"Yes, well, you certainly have every reason to do so." His gaze remained riveted straight ahead. "I'm an unsteady, moody fellow —and I nearly got you killed by drawing you into such terrible danger."

Another bright burst colored the black velvet sky with red and gold sparks.

"Actually, it was fun," murmured Harriet around the large lump that had formed in her throat. "We work well together. I shall... miss it."

I shall miss YOU.

"I don't suppose..."

Harriet held her breath as more fireworks exploded into the night.

"I don't suppose you would consider amending the original proposal," said Jack, after the *booms* had died away.

"That would depend on what you have in mind," she answered carefully.

"I was thinking..." He finally turned his head and the quiet fire in his eyes was infinitely brighter than any fancy display of pyrotechnics "...that perhaps you would consent to making the arrangement more permanent."

"Are you perchance asking me to marry you for real?"

Jack smiled. "That was the idea. I know you would like to have it all wrapped up in flowery words. But I'm not very romantic—"

Harriet cut off the rest of his words with a fierce hug. "Yes," she said simply.

His arms wrapped around her and suddenly she was floating on air. "A wise decision." His breath tickled lightly against her ear. "Otherwise you would have been subjected to some truly awful poetry, my love."

"I shall make you recite it at some point, but for now I would rather you repeat the last word you just said."

"You mean 'love'?"

"I just want to be sure I heard you correctly," murmured Harriet.

"Then I shall say it again. Love. I love you, Harriet." Jack kissed her. "I shall shout to the Heavens if you wish."

"Not necessary," she responded, and then kissed him back. "I heard you perfectly."

"Nonetheless, I shall say it again." His face softened, his gaze turning warm as melted chocolate. "I love you, Harriet. For years I've been wandering in the dark, but my heart has brought me back to the light of my life."

"I love you, Jack," she whispered, and then simply held him close, feeling no need to say anything more.

"*Ahem.*"

Harriet looked up just as James let out another long huff. "The fireworks have ended," he pointed out.

"But our journey together is just beginning," murmured Jack, just loud enough for her to hear. He took her hand. "Yes, yes, we're coming."

CHAPTER 18

Harriet undid the strings of her bonnet and set it on the side table of Lady Catherine's entrance foyer. It was a great relief to be back to her normal activities. The last two days had passed in such a helter-pelter that her head was still spinning—several private meetings with the Foreign Office and her father, time spent calming her harried household, and a number of quiet visits from Jack to begin making plans for the wedding...

With a guilty start, she realized she had not yet had a chance to tell Theo about all that had happened at Vauxhall Gardens. It would, of course, have to be a highly edited version. Some of the details would have to remain government secrets. But the state of her own heart was something she was looking forward to sharing with her dear friend.

Turning from the table, Harriet found herself pulled into a subtle hug from Mrs. Currough.

"I am so relieved to see you safe and sound," murmured the Irish Beauty. "Beaumont told me that all was well, and Leete was kind enough to send around a note the following day—along with a very lovely bracelet. But still, it is good to see for myself that you are unharmed."

The words were spoken with her usual discretion, however Miss Breville's ears were still just as sharp as her mind.

"Unharmed?" she repeated loudly. "What sort of dangerous adventures have you been up to, Miss Farnum?"

"Oh, none to speak of," she replied lightly.

"Just thwarting a cadre of deadly French spies," drawled Mrs. Currough. "With the help of the dashing Lord Leete and his friend Lord Osborne."

"*What!*" exclaimed Theo, who had just entered the townhouse, with Miss Ashmun and Mrs. Griffin trailing close behind her.

"*How—*"

"*Where—*"

Suddenly all the ladies began talking at once.

Lady Catherine quickly quieted everyone with several sharp raps of the heavy silver pastry platter. "It seems that perhaps we should defer discussion of Mrs. Wollstonecraft's essay to next week, seeing as no one will pay the least attention until we have heard all the exciting details."

"I can't tell you everything," apologized Harriet. "Certain things must remain confidential."

"*Sit,*" ordered Theo. "And tell us what you can."

She dutifully followed her friend to the drawing room and took a seat beside her.

"I knew I should not have cried off from the duc's party," said Theo with a sigh. "Was Osborne really involved in the heroics?" she added in a whisper.

Harriet nodded. "He played an integral role in capturing the villains."

"Oh." Looking a little crestfallen, Theo plucked at the sash of her gown. "I am not surprised to hear it. I wish..."

"Quiet, please!" called Lady Catherine.

The talking ceased as the members of the group all edged forward expectantly in their chairs.

With that, Harriet was given the signal to begin. "There is not all that much to tell," she said. "It was mostly going over documents and checking transfer manifests on my part, which really isn't very dashing or daring..."

～

"WHERE ARE WE GOING?" asked James as he followed Jack down the front steps of White's and out to the waiting carriage.

"To Covent Gardens."

"Hells bells, it's bad enough that your cousin Rafe shops for vegetables and fruits. Don't tell me you developed a taste for cooking, too?"

"No, I shall leave haute cuisine to him. I have other purchases in mind."

"What then?"

"You shall see shortly."

James did not manage to wrangle a more detailed answer during the short ride. Still grumbling, he followed Jack up through a narrow, shadowed passageway and shortly emerged into the bright glare of the market square and its riots of colors, shouts and smells.

"This way," said Jack, guiding his friend around a display of Seville oranges and marcona almonds. Winding their way through the narrow aisles of produce and kitchenwares, they crossed between the barrows of two meat pie vendors and turned into an area filled with a profusion of fragrant flowers and exotic blooms.

James looked in consternation as Jack halted and fell into negotiations with the proprietor of the largest stall. "Flowers?" he muttered.

"Yes, flowers," answered Jack. After another short discussion, the merchant began assembling a large bouquet of blooms ranging from buttery yellow and pale peach to coppery orange and burnt crimson.

"Harriet favors those hues," he murmured. "And for Mrs. Currough, I think we should have a range of blues and violets."

James made a face. "What the devil makes you say that?"

"Blue complements her hair and eye color," replied Jack. He waggled a brow. "Surely you are aware that noticing such things pleases a lady. One should also pay attention to what colors she favors in her clothing, as that also provides an excellent hint."

"Unlike you, I'm not lovestruck enough to care about pleasing a lady," muttered James. And yet his gaze seemed to stray to the array of cut flowers, which were arranged in groupings of similar hues.

Jack grinned. "Don't look so green around the gills. The prick of Cupid's arrow isn't quite as bad as you think." Indeed, rather than being a sore, festering wound, the bolt of love had spread a rippling of joy through his being. It had come slowly at first, then crested like a wave as he realized that he couldn't live without her.

"I shall take your word for it," retorted James. "I assure you, my hide is far thicker than yours."

"Ha!" was all he said in reply. Turning back to the merchant, he ordered a number of other bouquets in a variety of cheerful colors.

"What the devil are all those for?" demanded James, who seemed to be growing more uncomfortable by the moment.

"We are about to make a Grand Gesture." Jack thrust a half dozen of the paper-wrapped flowers into his friend's arms.

"Ye gods, you expect me to join you in appearing a Grand Fool?"

Tapping at his chin, Jack made a last survey of the fluttering colors. "What hues do you think Theo would like?"

Silence hung in the breeze for several moments before James

drew in a deep inhale and grudgingly replied. "A selection of pastels pinks, dotted with a few deeper shades of rose."

Jack held back a teasing comment as the merchant hurriedly assembled a lovely assortment of the requested colors. After paying for the purchases, he carefully took up the rest of the bundles. "Let's be off, before all these magnificent blooms wilt."

"Or before my courage withers on the vine," muttered James. "Dare I ask where we are taking these?"

"It's a Grand Surprise."

HARRIET WENT ON HALTINGLY with her story, uncomfortable at being the center of attention. And as the events unfolded, she found herself wincing inwardly on several occasions. In retrospect, she was lucky to have dodged disaster. She had made a number of rash mistakes.

However, the others seemed less critical of her faults.

"Good heavens!" exclaimed Lady Catherine when she finished recounting what had happened on the night of the masquerade. "That's far more exciting than any horrid novel."

"I daresay I would have swooned on the spot had some murderous French spy abducted me," chirped Miss Ashmun.

"Like all of our group, you are far too sensible to swoon," said Harriet decisively. "When faced with danger, you would have kept your wits about you." She slanted a grateful look at the Irish beauty. "Without Mrs. Currough's aid, things might not have worked out so well. As usual, she was observant at the party. And because she was clever enough to recall that the pleasure pavilion had been mentioned as a favorite haunt of the French, she was able to lead Lord Leete to the place."

"Aye," agreed Mrs. Griffin. "But you were clever too, recognizing the villain's face from the locket." She pursed her lips in thought. "So a woman was part of the conspirators."

Harriet nodded. "One of the leaders, in fact."

"Well, we all know the female intellect is capable of complex reasoning. But it is a pity to see it put to evil."

The others all nodded.

Mrs. McNulty had been listening in rapt silence to the story, but now, as the account trailed off, she ventured a gusty sigh. "Yes, it is very sad. Thank goodness you emerged unscathed, Harriet." Another sigh. "I daresay the same can't be said for your costume. It's a shame you didn't get to appear at the party for just a short while. You looked like a fairytale princess."

"The damage was quite minor," Harriet assured her. "A few snags and tears that my maid tells me will be easily mended."

"I am glad to hear it. Though I can't imagine you will have much call to wear it in the future."

"Oh, do describe it to us!" begged Miss Ashmun.

"Words can't possibly do it justice," replied Harriet.

The rest of the group tried to mask their disappointment.

"So I shall just wait and let you all see it for yourselves. The Duke of Pierpont wishes to hold a ball in celebration of the upcoming nuptials, and Lord Leete and I have decided to make it a masquerade. And you are all invited."

A flurry of excited titters ran around the room.

"Surely you can't mean *all*," murmured Mrs. Currough. "I am considered an impure woman, unwelcome in Polite Society."

"And despite my fancy French name, to the *ton* I am a mere laborer who toils in trade," piped up Mrs. McNulty.

"You are my friends," said Harriet firmly. "All of you. That is the only thing that matters to me and to Leete."

Mrs. McNulty's eyes lit up with a dreamy light. "I shall see a real Mayfair ballroom, all aglitter with sparkling chandeliers and bejeweled ladies?"

"Yes—and you shall sip French champagne and dance until dawn," said Theo.

"Fancy that," said the dressmaker in an awed tone. She

thought for a moment, then her face wreathed in a beatific smile. "I shall, of course, make costumes for everyone!"

The announcement elicited another round of enthusiasm, causing the decibel level in the room to rise sharply.

"Come, come, let us not all speak at once," said Lady Catherine, trying to restore some semblance of order. "I suggest we—"

Her voice was overwhelmed by a commotion at the front door. Much thumping and shuffling ensued. Harriet thought she caught a low oath as well. And then, oddly enough, a tantalizing floral scent suddenly perfumed the air.

She gave an experimental sniff. *Yes, definitely flowers.*

Catching Lady Catherine's eye, she raised a brow, but her hostess appeared equally mystified.

The puzzle was quickly resolved as Jack staggered into the room, bearing an armload of gaily-wrapped bouquets. James—*was it James?*—was right behind him, struggling to repress a bout of sneezing.

Her gaze went back to Jack, whose face was barely visible above the tops of several dusky pink peonies. "Well, um, this is quite a surprise."

He put all but one of the bouquets down on the side settee. "I wish to thank you and all your friends for being such singularly remarkable females," he announced loudly.

"It is," explained James, "a Grand Gesture."

With a flourishing bow, Jack presented her with the flowers. "I chose the colors for you," he murmured, dropping to a bended knee so his lips were hovering close to hers. "Reds, russets and bronzes to compliment your glorious hair."

"I keep telling you my hair is quite unremarkable."

He smiled. "You know how much I adore arguing with you."

Harriet couldn't manage a retort. The beauty of the blooms had her throat too tight for speech.

"I hope you like them," he said after another heartbeat of silence.

"I—I love them."

The tentative look in his eyes gave way to a deeper rippling of emotion. "Nothing makes me happier than to hear the word 'love' from your lips."

"In that case, let me say it again." She lowered her voice to a petal-soft whisper. "I love you."

A collective sigh seemed to flutter up from those closest to them as Jack rose. He chose one of the other bouquets and gallantly presented it to Mrs. Currough.

"A very small token of my thanks," he said.

The Irish Beauty dropped a very graceful curtsey. "You," she murmured, "are a very lucky man."

"Luckier than I deserve," he replied.

She regarded him with an appraising stare, then angled a wink at Harriet. "I think luck is equally matched between the two of you."

Jack's next bundle of flowers was bestowed on Mrs. McNulty, whose salty humor seemed to desert her on unwrapping the bold blaze of crimson and wine-red roses.

"You are an artist with silk and satin," he murmured. "You must promise to make Harriet's wedding dress."

"Y-You may count on it, milord."

Theo leaned over to whisper in Harriet's ear. "I didn't realize Jack had such a flair for the dramatic."

"Nor did I," she answered. A light-hearted inner imp appeared to have banished the shadow-dark inner demon. He seemed happier, more carefree.

Love did make the spirit feel as if it was dancing on a sugar-spun cloud, she mused.

Theo was about to speak again when James shuffled up and awkwardly handed her a bouquet. "These are for you," he said gruffly. "Harriet is very fortunate to have such a stalwart friend. The two of you were very clever and resourceful to draw out the French villains."

"You are right—she is the very best of friends," murmured Harriet as she watched Theo's cheeks turn the same vivid fuchsia hue as the dahlia crowning her arrangement.

"T-Thank you," Theo stammered.

"You are welcome," said James gravely.

"Harriet has told us how wonderfully brave you were in helping to rescue her," said Theo, recovering her equilibrium. "I thank you for that as well."

James seemed uncomfortable with the praise. "I did nothing but follow Jack's plan. Any clodpole could have done it." A summons from Jack saved him from having to go on. "I had better help with passing out the rest of the bouquets."

"Flowers for all of us?" exclaimed Miss Breville. She took off her spectacles and polished them on her sleeve before taking a closer look. "They are exquisite. But whatever are they for, sir?"

"For being steadfast friends and kindred spirits," answered Jack. "I have come to see that the strictures of the *ton* are awfully confining for a female who is inquisitive and intelligent. And so I am glad Harriet has a group with whom she can speak her mind and discuss ideas that interest her, however radical they may be."

He fixed Harriet with a look that sent a shiver of heat skating down her spine. "I, on the other hand, am not nearly so admirable as she is. But she makes me want to be better than I think I can be."

There was a soft rustling of fabric as several members of the group surreptitiously drew out their handkerchiefs.

"You surprise me, sir," said Lady Catherine, challenging Jack with a show of blunt cynicism. "I had heard you were a superficial fribble. But the gossips seem misinformed."

He gave a rueful smile. "I surprise myself."

"Only because you look at yourself in a far harsher light than anyone else does," said Harriet as she rose and came to loop her arm through his.

"It is quite true that shadows can distort the view," observed

Lady Catherine. "I have a feeling that in the future, you will not often find yourself cast in the shade."

"The future does look bright," he said, drawing Harriet closer. As she watched the afternoon sun play off the glass of the diamond-paned windows, she couldn't help but agree.

The clock chimed the hour, signaling the end of the meeting, and they moved to a quiet spot by the bookshelves as the others gathered up their belongings and headed for the front door.

"Lady Catherine's neighbors will think she has formed a garden club," quipped Jack as the last of the members thanked him and left with her bouquet of colorful blooms.

"That was very thoughtful of you," said Theo, who had lingered behind. "And very romantic. Lord Byron would be green with envy."

Jack gave a mock shudder. "You may be sure that I will *not* be penning poetry or any such argy-bargy nonsense."

"No poetry will be required. But flowers on occasion will be welcome," said Harriet.

"That I can manage." He shifted his stance. "Is your carriage waiting?"

She nodded.

"Then perhaps I might ride home with you. There are several things we need to discuss about the wedding plans."

Harriet still felt at times as if she had been swept up into some enchanted fairytale and her handsome prince might disappear in a puff of smoke at any moment.

But then, Jack's reassuring warmth in moments such as these would remind her that he was wonderfully real.

"I would like that very much," she answered.

Turning to James, he called, "My coachman will drop you back at White's."

James signaled his assent. "But first, I ought to escort Lady Theo to her carriage. This is not quite as genteel an area as Mayfair."

Harriet and Jack allowed their friends to leave first, then followed at a more leisurely pace.

"Do you think..." mused Jack, watching the couple turn down one of the side streets.

Harriet thought for a moment. "I am not sure. Theo has yet to unfurl all her new blossoms, and James... well, I am not certain James knows his own heart. I suppose only time will tell."

"Wise words, as always." He slipped his arm around her waist, and they crossed the square in companionable silence. On the far side, however, he came to an abrupt halt. "It was here, on this very spot, that our paths first crossed to begin this adventure."

"It was hardly an auspicious start—you knocked me over."

"Actually, we argued about who knocked whom." He chuckled. "Though I think I knew deep down inside that I had fallen head over heels."

"You took your time in showing it."

"Well, as to that..." Jack leaned down to brush a swift kiss to her lips. "Good things come to those who wait."

The devilish twinkle in his eyes made her heart leap. She clasped his hand, entwining her fingers with his.

"I can think of several other aphorisms—including better late than never. However, I shall simply say you are a very good thing indeed."

"Then kiss me again, my love."

"I should make you wait." Harriet smiled. "But I won't."

ALSO BY ANDREA PICKENS

TRADITIONAL REGENCIES

INTREPID HEROINES

The Banished Bride

The Storybook Hero

Second Chances

A Stroke of Luck

A Lady of Letters

The Defiant Governess

The Major's Mistake

Code of Honor

The Hired Hero

Pistols At Dawn

DANGEROUS LIASIONS

A Diamond in the Rough

Sweeter than Sin

Devil May Care

REGENCY SPY/ADVENTURE/ROMANCES

MRS. MERLIN'S ACADEMY FOR EXTRAORDINARY YOUNG LADIES

The Spy Wore Silk

Seduced by a Spy

The Scarlet Spy

To Love a Spy

OTHER

Omnibus

Christmas by Candlelight

ABOUT THE AUTHOR

I started creating books at the age of five, or so my mother tells me. And she has the proof—a neatly penciled story, the pages lavishly illustrated with full color crayon drawings of horses and bound with staples—to back up her claim. I have since moved on from Westerns to writing about Regency England (clearly I have a thing for Men In Boots!) a time and place that has captured my imagination ever since I opened the covers of Jane Austen's "Pride and Prejudice."

I have a BA and an MFA in Graphic Design from Yale University, where I studied book design (As you see, I've always had a left brain-right brain love affair with art and the printed word.) These days, when I'm not tethered to my keyboard I enjoy traveling to interesting destinations around the world—however, my favorite spot is London, where the esoteric museums, funky antique markets and used book stores offer a wealth of inspiration for my stories.